應用英文寫作系列之一

Writing Effective Study Plans

有效撰寫英文讀書計劃

By Ted Knoy

柯泰德

Illustrated by Yang Jin Yao

插圖 ： 楊錦堯

清 蔚 科 技 出 版

Ted Knoy is also author of the following books in the Chinese Technical Writers Series *(科技英文寫作系列)*:

An English Style Approach for Chinese Technical Writers
精通科技論文（ 報告 ）寫作之捷徑

English Oral Presentations for Chinese Technical Writers
作好英語會議簡報

A Correspondence Manual for Chinese Technical Writers
英文信函參考手册

An Editing Workbook for Chinese Technical Writers
科技英文編修訓練手册

Advanced Copyediting Practice for Chinese Technical Writers
科技英文編修訓練手册－進階篇

謹以此書獻給我的岳父黃國榮先生與岳母周梅雀女士

序言

科技創新迅速，國家競爭力需要不斷提昇，尤其當我國正積極準備加入各種世界組織之際，人才養成特別重要。國家的發展需要專業人才，而專業人才需要更精深的學習再造。有效撰寫讀書計劃一書主旨在提供國人精深學習前的準備，包括：讀書計劃及推薦信函的建構、完成。籍由本書中視覺化訊息的互動及練習，國人可以更明確的掌握全篇的意涵，及更完整的表達心中的意念。這也是本書異於坊間同類書籍只著重在片斷記憶，不求理解最大之處。

同時本書也結合了「精確寫作」及「明白寫作」的精華，這二者同時是科技英文寫作訓練手册及其進階篇的核心，如今與讀書計劃撰寫呵成一氣，更可以避免及糾正國人常犯的寫作格式錯誤，快速提昇國人英文寫作及編修技巧。

希望國人經由本書的訓練，可以更順利的展開精深學習的計劃。如同之前所述，專業人才是國家的希望，提昇國家競爭力應是全體國人的目標及責任。

于樹偉 主任
工業技術研究院
環境與安全衛生技術發展中心

序言

柯泰德先生致力於提昇國人英文寫作能力不餘遺力，除了在國立清華大學及交通大學開設科技英文寫作課程之外，更前後出版了五本「科技英文寫作系列」叢書， 如今加上「應用英文寫作系列」的第一本書，書名是『有效撰寫讀書計劃』，使得英文的寫作更爲積極、實用。

『有效撰寫讀書計劃』主要是針對想要進階學習的讀者，由基本的自我學習經驗描述延伸至未來目標的設定，更進一步強調推薦信函的撰寫，籍由圖片式訊息互動，讓讀者主動聯想及運用寫作知識及技巧，避免一味的記憶零星的範例；如此一來，讀者可以更清楚表明個別的特質及快速掌握重點。同時本書也加入科技英文寫作系列叢書的精華部份，強調「精確寫作」及「明白寫作」，讓讀者學習自行編修的技巧。

有效撰寫讀書計劃是進階學習的第一步，也是非常關鍵重要的一步，一個清楚，切中要點的讀書計劃絕對是成功進階學習的跳板。

王玫 組長
工業研究技術院／ 化學工業研究所
企劃與技術推廣組

Table of Contents

Foreword

Professional writing is essential to garner international recognition of Taiwan's commercial and technological achievements. To meet this requirement, "The Chinese Professional Writers Series" seeks to provide a sound English writing curriculum and, on a more practical level, to provide valuable reference guides for Chinese professionals. The Series supports Chinese professional writers in the following areas:

Writing style

The books in this Series seek to transform archaic ways of writing into a more active and direct writing style which makes the author's main ideas easier to identify.

Structure and content

Another issue facing professional writers is how to organize the structure and contents of reports and other common forms of writing. The exercises in this Workbook will help writers to avoid and correct stylistic errors that are commonly found in study plans intended for advanced study.

Quality

Inevitably, writers prepare reports to meet the expectations of editors, referees/reviewers, as well as to satisfy journal requirements. The books in this Series are prepared with these specific needs in mind.

Writing Effective Study Plans is the first book in the Chinese Professional Writers Series.

前言

『Writing Effective Study Plans』為「應用英文寫作系列（The Chinese Professional Writers Series）」之第一本書，本書中練習題部份主要是幫助國人進階學習的申請及避免，糾正常犯寫作格式上錯誤，由反覆練習中，進而熟能生巧提升寫作及編修能力。

「應用英文寫作系列」將針對以下內容逐步協助國人解決在英文寫作上所遭遇之各項問題：

A.寫作型式：把往昔通常習於抄襲的寫作方法轉換成更積極主動的寫作方式，俾使讀者所欲表達的主題意念更加清楚。更進一步糾正國人寫作口語習慣。

B.方法型式：指出國內寫作者從事英文寫作或英文翻譯時常遇到的文法問題。

C.內容結構：將寫作的內容以下面的方式結構化：目標、一般動機、個人動機。並了解不同的目的和動機可以影響報告的結構，由此，獲得最適當的報告內容。

D.內容品質：以編輯、審查委員的要求來寫作此一系列之書籍，以滿足讀者的英文要求。

Introduction

This writing workbook aims to instruct students that are preparing for advanced study on how to write a simple, concise and straightforward study plan. The following elements of an effective study plan are introduced: expressing interest in a field of study, displaying knowledge of that field, describing academic background and achievements, introducing research and professional experiences, describing extracurricular activities relevant to study, describing personal qualities relevant to study, outlining career objectives, and stating why an institution was selected for advanced study. This workbook also describes how to write an effective recommendation letter for advanced study.

Chinese writers often express concern over their inability to improve their English writing skills, citing that they quickly target new words, phrases or patterns after learning them. Part of this problem comes from over relying on words within a text without understanding its practical meaning. Without a practical context, students only memorize words, which are forgotten easily. Therefore, this workbook does not contain an enumerated list on how to write a study plan. Nor does this book overly emphasize samples so that readers only need to copy phrases contained herein (although samples are provided at the end of each unit). Alternatively, this workbook visually represents the information required to write effective study plans and advanced study recommendations. In doing so, students must understand the context of the information and then use it appropriately.

Each unit begins with four visually represented situations that provide essential information for students to write a specific aspect of a study plan or recommendation. Additional written activities that are related to those four situations allow students to understand how the visual representation relates to the ultimate goal of compiling an effective application. Copyediting exercises also train students to edit their own writing for conciseness and clarity. An Answer Key makes this book ideal for classroom use. For instance, to test a student's listening comprehension, a teacher can first read the text that describes the situations for a particular unit. Either individually or in small groups, students can work through the exercises to produce a simple, yet concise study plan and recommendation letter.

簡介

本書主要針對想進階學習的學生，指導其如何撰寫精簡切中要點的讀書計劃。書中內容包括：1. 表達學習領域興趣 2. 展現已有的學習領域知識 3. 描述學歷背景及已獲成就 4. 介紹研究及工作經驗 5. 描述與學習有關的課外活動 6. 描述與學習有關的個人特質 7. 概述未來工作目標 8. 解釋選擇該校原由 9. 撰寫推薦信函（ A 部份 ）推薦信函開始及推薦人的資格 10. 撰寫推薦信函（ B 部份 ）被推薦人與進階學習有關的個人特質及信函結尾 。

國人英文寫作太過依賴片斷的字詞而忽略了全篇的實際意涵，因此本書並不打算條列式的告訴讀者如何撰寫讀書計劃，也不過份強調範例的模倣。而是更多元化的提供與寫作相關的視覺訊息，讓國人能更深刻的瞭解訊息的內容及更正確的使用他們撰寫讀書計劃。

本書中的每個單元呈現四個視覺化的情境，提供國人讀書計劃及推薦信函寫作實質訊息，而相關附加的寫作練習讓讀者做實際的訊息運用。此外，書中的編修訓練同時加強讀者精確寫作及明白寫作的技巧。同時本書也非常適合在課堂上使用。不管是讀者個人自修或是團體使用，書中結合視覺訊息的練習可以讓國人建構一個精簡有效的讀書計劃或推薦信函。

Copy editing marks used in this Workbook

修改前句子	修改後句子	修改符號的代表意義
fieldd of study	field of study	Delete 刪除
Apply apply for study.	Apply for study.	
current knowledge Display of field.	Display current knowledge of field.	Insert 插入文字
current knowledge Display of field.	Display current knowledge of field.	
# Describeextracurricularactivities.	Describe extracurricular activities.	Insert space 插入空格
Describeextracurricularactivities.	Describe extracurricular activities.	
Statement of Purpose	statement of purpose	Lower case 大寫改成小寫
STATEMENT OF PURPOSE	statement of purpose	
indiana university	Indiana University	Capitals 小寫改成大寫
mit	MIT	
Oultine carere objectives.	Outline career objectives.	Transpose 前後對調
career Outline objectives.	Outline career objectives.	
for study, Recommend a student	Recommend a student for study.	Brackets 括號
Summarize your experiences	Summarize your experiences.	Period 句

Unit One

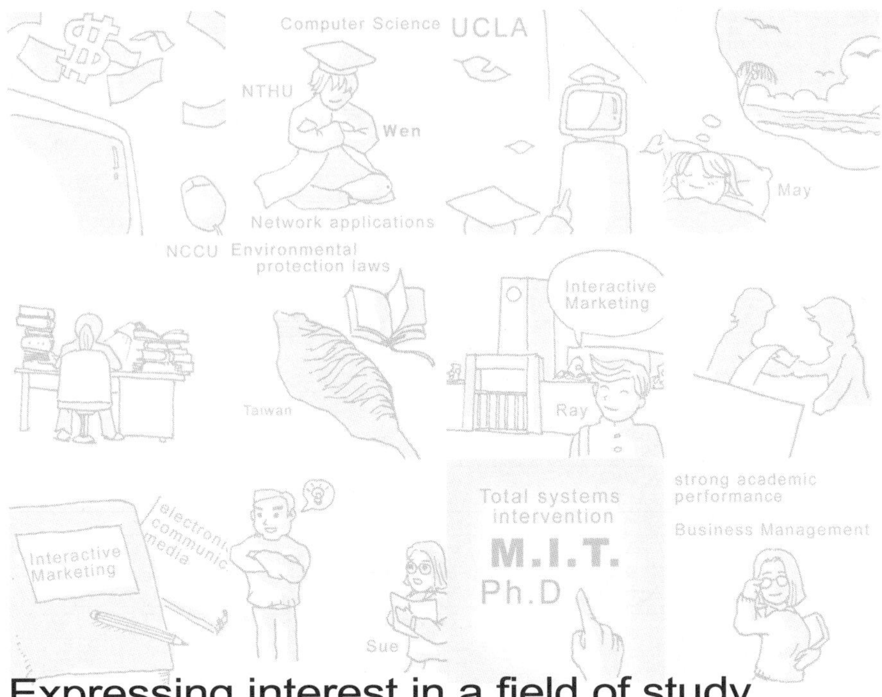

Expressing interest in a field of study

表達學習領域興趣

Vocabulary and related expressions

a concentration in 主攻
premier 有名的
acquired 拿到
implement 執行
immersing 埋首於
administrative 行政的
recently emerging 新興的
intrigued 著迷
ensure 確定
distinguished 著名的
renowned 有名的
strong academic background 強有力的學歷背景
solid background 強有力的個人背景
rigorous challenges 嚴厲的挑戰

1 >>
Computer Science
NTHU
Wen
Network applications
UCLA
2 >>
May
NCCU
Environmental
protection laws
Taiwan
3 >>
Interactive
Marketing
Ray
Interactive
Marketing
4 >>
Sue
Total systems
intervention
M.I.T.
Ph.D
strong academic
performance
Business Management

A Write down the key points to the situations on the preceding page while the instructor reads the script on page 170 aloud.

Situation 1

____

____

____

Situation 2

____

____

____

Situation 3

____

____

____

Situation 4

____

____

____

B Write three questions beginning with *What* based on the four situations in this unit and answer them.

Examples

What topic is Wen fascinated with?

He is fascinated with the Internet's impact on all aspects of modern commerce.

What would May like her graduate school research to center on?

How the government can implement environmentally friendly practices.

1. ______________________________

____

2. ______________________________

____

3. ______________________________

____

C **Write three questions beginning with *Which* based on the four situations in this unit and answer them.**

Examples

Which topic has Ray studied since high school?

Marketing.

Which university would Sue like to attend for her doctoral studies?

She would like to attend MIT for her doctoral studies.

1. ______________________________

____

2. ______________________________

____

3. ______________________________

____

D Write questions that match the answers provided.

Examples

How long has May dreamed of a world free of pollution?

Since childhood

What is a timely topic for the recently emerging electronic communications media in Taiwan?

Interactive marketing research

1. ______________________________

Organizational processes, design, and culture

2. ______________________________

National Tsing Hua University

3. ______________________________

How the government can implement environmentally friendly practices

E In the space below, describe your interest in a field of study.

____

____

____

____

____

____

Writing for Conciseness: Use Active Voice Frequently

常用主動語氣

A simple way to delete the length of a sentence and make it direct at the same time is to frequently use the active voice. Switching from passive voice to active voice often makes a sentence more direct, concise and persuasive. Whereas sentences using passive voice tend to be wordy or indecisive, sentences utilizing active voice make the technical document more immediate and concise.

就像先前所說，如何用最少的字來表達一個完整的意念通常是科技寫作者一個大挑戰，然而這裡有一個祕訣，那就是使用主動語法。請記住主動語氣使句子更直接，明確及更有說服力。

Consider the following examples:

Original
Selection of qualified candidates is made by the admissions committee by carefully reviewing application materials.

Revised
The admissions committee selects qualified candidates by carefully reviewing application materials.

Original

Sufficient computer skills to build a web site is possessed by many individuals.

Revised

Many individuals possess sufficient computer skills to build a web site.

The above revisions demonstrate that in addition to making the sentences shorter, the verb expresses a clearer action than in the original ones. Therefore, using active voice often makes the document easier to read.

以上修正部份除了使原句簡短外，動詞更爲清楚。所以使用主動語氣會使整篇文章更明朗。

However, passive voice is preferred when the doer of the action is unknown or unimportant (or less important than the action itself). Consider the following example:

然而，有些情況卻要使用被動語氣，通常是行爲者不明或是不重要時。請細想比較以下例句：

The graduate school applicants are notified of the outcome of their submissions within a reasonable time.

In the above sentence, who notifies ***The graduate school applicants of the outcome of their submissions*** is unknown or unimportant, and definitely less important than the action of the graduate students being notified. Therefore, in this instance, passive voice is preferred.

在此句中，使用電腦軌跡球的人不知是誰也不重要，重點是球移動的這個事件，所以您知道在這情況下要使用被動語法。

Time is needed to make a careful decision.

Similar to the above example, the person who needs time is unknown or important, and definitely less important than the action of needing time to move a careful decision.

類似以上的例句，需要這個空間的人不知道是誰也並不重要，重點應放在移動球所需空間的這個事件上，故要使用被動語法。

Nevertheless, switching from passive voice to active voice makes the sentence more direct, concise and persuasive.

F Put the following sentences in active voice by using the copyediting marks on page 14.

1. A major market for Taiwanese products in the near future will obviously be provided by China's population of over 1 billion people.

2. Heavy dependence on exports is a characteristic feature of Taiwan's economy.

3. Intervention in stock market fluctuations is often made by the Taiwanese government.

4. Strong analytical skills of applicants is a heavy emphasis of graduate school admission committees.

5. Careful screening of all candidates is made by the admissions committee.

6. Long term damage may be caused by these harmful practices.

7. Development of sound fiscal policies by our nation's economists is necessary.

8. Keeping abreast of the latest changes in regulations and technological innovations is of essential concern to economists.

9. Integrating knowledge in research and policy in the multi-disciplinary field of human development is rare in graduate programs in Taiwan.

10. The software may be difficult for users without a computer background to install.

G Consider the following examples of how to express interest in a field of study:

I have long been intrigued by creative, strategic decision making. This careful selection of which methods to adopt and actions to enforce in order to ensure that the best decision is made is what will make me a successful business manager. If admitted to your program, I intend to concentrate on total systems intervention, including related issues of organizational processes, design, and culture. This explains why I chose Columbia University for doctoral studies. In addition to a distinguished Business Administration program, your renowned research in contemporary management strategies such as business process re-engineering, quality management and total systems intervention is widely recognized. My strong academic performance and solid background in Business Management have prepared me to meet the rigorous challenges of your program.

~~~~ * ~~~~ * ~~~~ * ~~~~ * ~~~~

I would like to build upon my solid academic training and relevant work experiences by pursuing a Ph.D. in Electrical Engineering.
~~~~

~~~~~ * ~~~~~ * ~~~~~ * ~~~~~ * ~~~~~

During my upcoming graduate studies, I look forward to absorbing enormous amounts of new information that is not related directly to my course requirements. I believe that my creativity and unique perspectives will contribute positively to any research team, regardless of whether we are engaging in case studies or undertaking research projects.

~~~~~ * ~~~~~ * ~~~~~ * ~~~~~ * ~~~~~

Education is a life long pursuit. Throughout our lives, we are constantly exposed to learning opportunities, regardless of whether it is a special event, gesture, or small sign. While uncertainty makes our lives both challenging and fulfilling, the following questions arise: How do we change? When is the critical time at which individuals change? How can we educate people within a conducive environment that matches their developmental processes? I am interested in answering these questions in graduate school.

~~~~~ * ~~~~~ * ~~~~~ * ~~~~~ * ~~~~~

Since childhood, I have always dreamed of a world free of pollution and pondered how environmentally conscious individuals can improve their surroundings. The strong research fundamentals acquired during my undergraduate years at National Cheng Chi University have prepared me for advanced study in Public Administration. My graduate school research will hopefully center on how the government can implement environmentally friendly practices. Furthermore, I plan to identify those governmental
~~~~~

measures that are vital to Taiwan's industrial sector. Moreover, I intend to actively participate in developing environmental protection laws for Taiwan.

~~~~~ * ~~~~~ * ~~~~~ * ~~~~~ * ~~~~~

I have studied Marketing since high school, immersing myself in customer service-related issues. I am especially interested in how administrative database systems are increasingly customer-oriented and how the customer and supplier are related. Thus, I wish to further my knowledge through graduate studies on interactive marketing research, which is a timely topic for the recently emerging electronic communications media in Taiwan.

~~~~~ * ~~~~~ * ~~~~~ * ~~~~~ * ~~~~~

I am fascinated with the Internet's impact on all aspects of modern commerce. This fascination has resulted in my near completion of a Master's degree in Computer Science with a concentration in network applications from National Tsing Hua University, one of our country's premier institutes of higher learning. Upon completion of this degree, I will immediately pursue a Ph.D. in the same field, hopefully at your renowned university.

~~~~~ * ~~~~~ * ~~~~~ * ~~~~~ * ~~~~~

From an early age, I have had much enthusiasm in handling small creatures, which prompted me to enroll in Veterinary Science courses as well as to submit this current application to the Graduate school of Animal Husbandry.
~~~~~

~~~~~~ * ~~~~~~ * ~~~~~~ * ~~~~~~ * ~~~~~~

I cannot fully describe the unique way in which Taiwanese art expresses a unique affection towards my country.

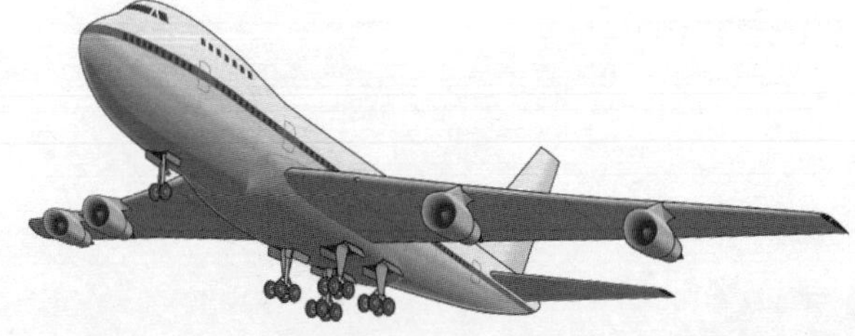
~~~~~~

Unit Two

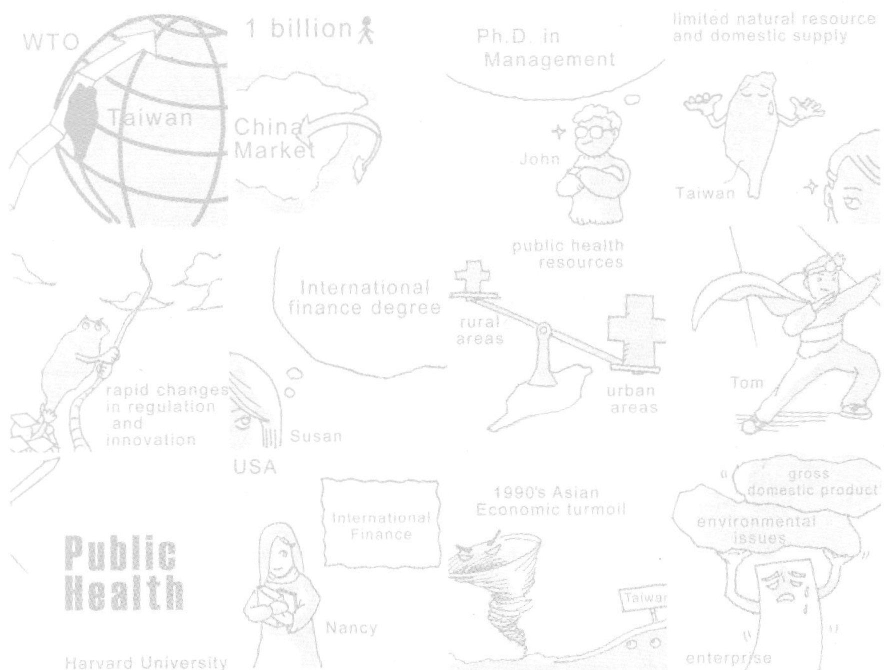

Displaying current knowledge of the field of study

展現已有的學習領域知識

（精確寫作:動詞代替名詞）

Vocabulary and related expressions

widely anticipated entry 廣被預期加入
witness unprecedented growth 目睹空前的經濟成長
logical extension 合理的延伸
commence 著手
aspiration 熱望
fluctuating 波動
pursue 追求
unequal distribution 不公平的分配
inadequate 不適當
remote 遙遠的
inferior 低級的
equitable 公平的
devote oneself to 把自己奉獻給
flourish 繁茂
as evidenced by 使成爲一個證據
economic turmoil 經濟風暴
relatively unscathed 相對來説沒有受到損失
strained entrepreneurial development 緊張的企業發展
enhance competitiveness 提高競爭

Unit Two Displaying current knowledge of a field of study

展現已有的學習領域知識（精確寫作:動詞代替名詞）

A **Write down the key points to the situations on the preceding page while the instructor reads the script on page 176 aloud.**

Situation 1

____

____

____

Situation 2

____

____

____

Situation 3

____

____

____

Situation 4

____

____

____

B **Write three questions beginning with *What* based on the four situations in this unit and answer them.**

Examples

What will China's population of over 1 billion people provide in the near future?

A major market for Taiwanese products.

What does Taiwan heavily depend on?

International trade.

1. ______________________________

____

2. ______________________________

____

3. ______________________________

____

C **Write three questions beginning with *Which* based on the four situations in this unit and answer them.**

Examples

Which areas are problematic for Taiwan?

Deregulation and globalization.

Which degree has Susan decided to pursue?
A graduate degree in
International Finance.

1. ____________________

____

2. ____________________

____

3. ____________________

____

D **Write questions that match the answers provided.**

Examples

What is essential for a productive and secure society?

Equitable health care

Which region does Taiwan hope to become the financial center?

The Asian Pacific

1. ______________________________

The Institute of Public Health at Harvard University

2. ______________________________

The way in which domestic companies can compete with multinational corporations

3. ______________________________

Yes

E In the space below, describe your current knowledge of the field of study.

____

____

____

____

____

____

Writing for Conciseness: Use Verbs Instead of Nouns

動詞代替名詞

Wordiness also comes from creating nouns out of verbs (known as nominalizations). This tendency leads to weak verbs, which will be further discussed in Unit Four. In addition, overusing nouns instead of verbs also creates needless prepositions. Consider the following examples:

句子冗贅的原因也可能是使用太多的名詞，通常這些名詞是由動詞轉化來的，而結果是使動詞更無力，此部份會在第四單元詳論。此外，過份的濫用名詞也帶來了多餘的介係詞。細想以下例句：

Original

Students must reach a decision on where to submit their graduate school applications.

Revised

Students must decide where to submit their graduate school applications.

Original

The laboratory technician conducted a simulation of the new program.

Revised
The laboratory technician simulated the new program.

Original
The applicants performed a survey of available graduate programs in engineering.

Revised
The applicants surveyed available graduate programs in engineering.

Other examples include

give consideration to	consider
reach a conclusion	conclude
undertake an investigation of	investigate
make a provision for	provide

F Correct the following sentences by using the copyediting marks on page 14.

1. Difficulty is faced in description of personal strengths to the admissions committee by applicants.

2. Recommendation of the applicant for graduate study is made by the department chairman.

3. A significant increase in the number of applicants to graduate school has occurred in recent years.

4. Knowledge of how the admissions procedure works is required by graduate school applicants.

5. Not only is the academic record of an applicant considered by the admissions committee, but execution of related procedures is performed by that same committee.

6. A recommendation of accepting Tom as a graduate student for pursuit of a doctorate degree in Finance was made by the committee chairman.

7. Selection of a career is achieved by an evaluation of available options.

8. An increase of career oprtunities occurs by enhancement of one's computer skills.

9. A stipulation by the admissions committee is that the forms be handed in by applicants no later than December 1st.

10. Awareness of the changing economic climate is a must for job applicants when looking for employment.

G **Look at the following examples of how to display your current knowledge of a field of study:**

Many individuals have the computer skills required to create a web site. However, despite tremendous promotion and employment of the latest information technologies, many commercial web sites have ceased operations. Therefore, I would like to pursue a Masters degree in Internet marketing to identify what products and services will succeed as well as the factors that attract visitors to a web site.

~~~~~ * ~~~~~ * ~~~~~ * ~~~~~ * ~~~~~

With Taiwan's widely anticipated entry into the World Trade Organization, undoubtedly, its economy will witness unprecedented growth and greater access to global markets. Moreover, China's population of over 1 billion people may provide a major market for Taiwanese products in the near future, thus offering endless possibilities for market expansion. These exciting times in the business world fuel my aspiration to attain a Ph.d. in Business Management as a logical basis with which to undertake a career in related research.

~~~~~ * ~~~~~ * ~~~~~ * ~~~~~ * ~~~~~

Taiwan heavily depends on international trade owing to its limited natural resources and domestic supply as well as demand in either the capital or commodity market. To fulfill its aspirations of becoming the financial center of the Asian Pacific region, Taiwan is facing deregulation and globalization. Taiwan is becoming more sensitive to fluctuating international markets, thus forging closer relations with other countries. Currently, Taiwan's most urgent need is for local economists to develop expert and comparative abilities, which match the rapid changes in regulation and innovation, such as those in the United States. Therefore, I have decided to pursue a graduate degree in International Finance.

~~~~~ * ~~~~~ * ~~~~~ * ~~~~~ * ~~~~~

The Taiwanese government often intervenes in stock market fluctuations, particularly during an unstable political climate. For instance, when a financial crisis occurs, the Government lowers banking charges and modifies their accounting practices. However, I am skeptical about the merits of such intervention. While financial markets become stabilized in the short term, these practices may result in long-term damage. I am interested in pursuing a Masters of Business Administration at your university to understand what measures should be adopted (if any) when a financial crisis occurs.

~~~~~ * ~~~~~ * ~~~~~ * ~~~~~ * ~~~~~

Comparing urban and rural areas, Taiwan has an unequal distribution of urban public health resources. In particular, inadequate teaching faculties and libraries in these remote areas result in fewer high school graduates as well as an inferior standard of medical care. Inadequate health care available in these areas is further evidenced in the prevalence of severe health problems such as alcoholism and various infectious diseases. Equitable health care is essential for a productive and secure society. This explains why I have decided to devote myself to effectively addressing public health issues in Taiwan following an advanced degree at the Institute of Public Health at Harvard University.

~~~~~ * ~~~~~ * ~~~~~ * ~~~~~ * ~~~~~

Taiwan's economy has flourished in recent decades, as evidenced by rapid industrial expansion and market deregulation. Although the island escaped the Asian economic turmoil of the late 1990s relatively unscathed, a surging gross domestic product as well as an increasing emphasis on environmental issues has strained entrepreneurial development. Growing up in such an economically dynamic environment has motivated my interest in researching how domestic companies can compete with multinational corporations and how our government can adjust financial market strategies to enhance local competitiveness. Moreover, as Taiwan faces the reconstruction of its financial markets, identifying appropriate deregulations is essential. Therefore, I have decided to complete a Masters degree in International Finance.
~~~~~

~~~~~ * ~~~~~ * ~~~~~ * ~~~~~ * ~~~~~

Early childhood is a critical period for later social development. This marks the beginning at which children must leave their parents for an environment totally alien from their own. To adjust, they must interact with peers who have backgrounds that may differ from their own. Alternatively, an increasing number of women are joining the labor force and their children are going to school at a younger age. Moreover, for Taiwanese parents who are overly concerned with their children's development, supplemental training is widely available to foster a child's academic and social development. While the demand for early childhood education is expanding in Taiwan, the quality and availability of teachers and institutions have yet to be standardized. Most institutional programmers and teachers focus on developing skills, regardless of the emotional or psychological makeup of the learners. Furthermore, few graduate programs in Taiwan integrate knowledge in research, practice and policy in the multi-disciplinary field of human development, with subsequent concentrations in early childhood education. I am therefore encouraged by your Human Development program, especially early childhood education, which your prestigious school offers.

~~~~~ * ~~~~~ * ~~~~~ * ~~~~~ * ~~~~~

In Taiwan, except with clinical or industrial occupations, psychology is viewed as a "theory" that attempts to account for phenomenon rather than actively implementing an educational policy for schools. However, Taiwanese students are extremely anxious over their grades to the extent that they attend supplementary school during weeknights and hire personal tutors - all in an effort to successfully pass the highly competitive senior high school or university entrance examinations. However, during this process, many fail to develop a motivation for learning, resulting in a decline in academic performance following program completion. I firmly believe that if our educational system could incorporate developmental processes, students would take a more active role in the field of interest. The Human Development and Education program at your prestigious school offers a starting point in my search to effectively address this obstacle.

~~~~~ * ~~~~~ * ~~~~~ * ~~~~~ * ~~~~~

Despite its small size, Taiwan has a rich architectural heritage, as evidenced in its temples, theaters, and residential and public buildings. However, the lack of a standard methodology and research environment regarding this topic prevented me from learning about Taiwanese architecture in a systematic manner during my youth. This explains why I became familiar with Western architecture at a relatively young age without fully appreciating our Island's proud architectural heritage. It was not until my undergraduate studies that I was introduced to Taiwanese arhitecture, gradually learning to appreciate it. I further became aware of the risks posed to the survival of Taiwanese architecture owing to the lack of a research
~~~~~

discipline as well as the dwindling number of artisans with the passing of each generation. To ensure that Taiwanese architecture survives, academic research in this field is essential. With my desire to pursue advanced study in this area, several professors in my department recommended your school owing to its excellent faculty and research environment.

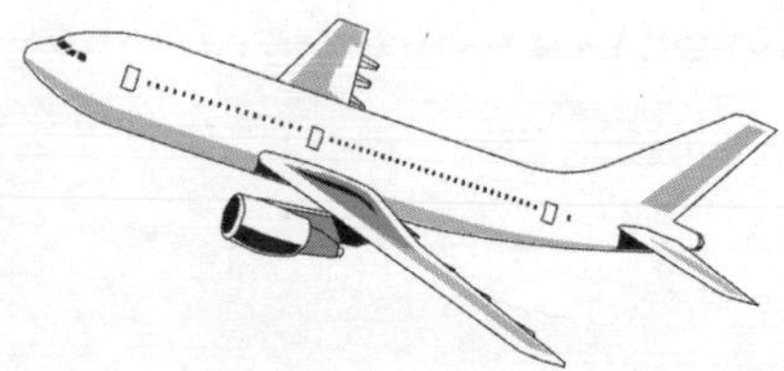

Unit Three

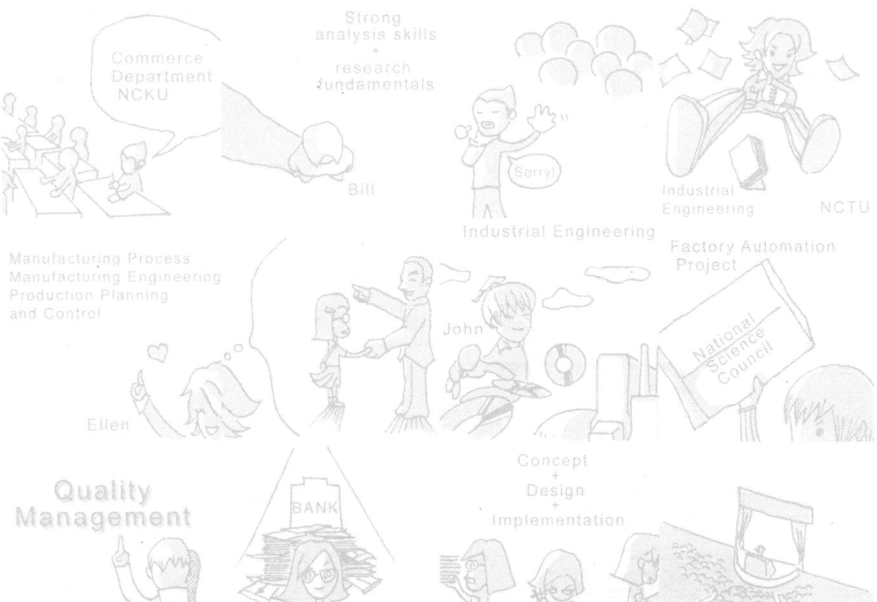

Describing academic background and achievements

描述學歷背景及已獲成就

Vocabulary and related expressions

highly competitive 高度競爭
nationwide university entrance examination 大學聯考
cumulative GPA (grade point average) 累積的四年平均成績
attest to 證明
strong analytical skills 強的分析能力
research fundamentals 研究的原則
refused 拒絕
equipped 配備
rigorous 嚴格的
premier 有名的
fundamental skills 基本的能力
come into contact with 接觸
departmental curricula 系上課程
theoretical and practical understanding 理論上和實際上的瞭解
solve problems logically 合理的解決問題
theoretical knowledge 理論的知識
practical laboratory experiences 實驗室經驗
fostered 培養
glimpse into 一瞥
dynamic nature 動力本性
fully engaging 完全接觸
considerable praise 相當多的讚揚

Unit Three Describing academic background and achievements 描述學歷背景及已獲成就

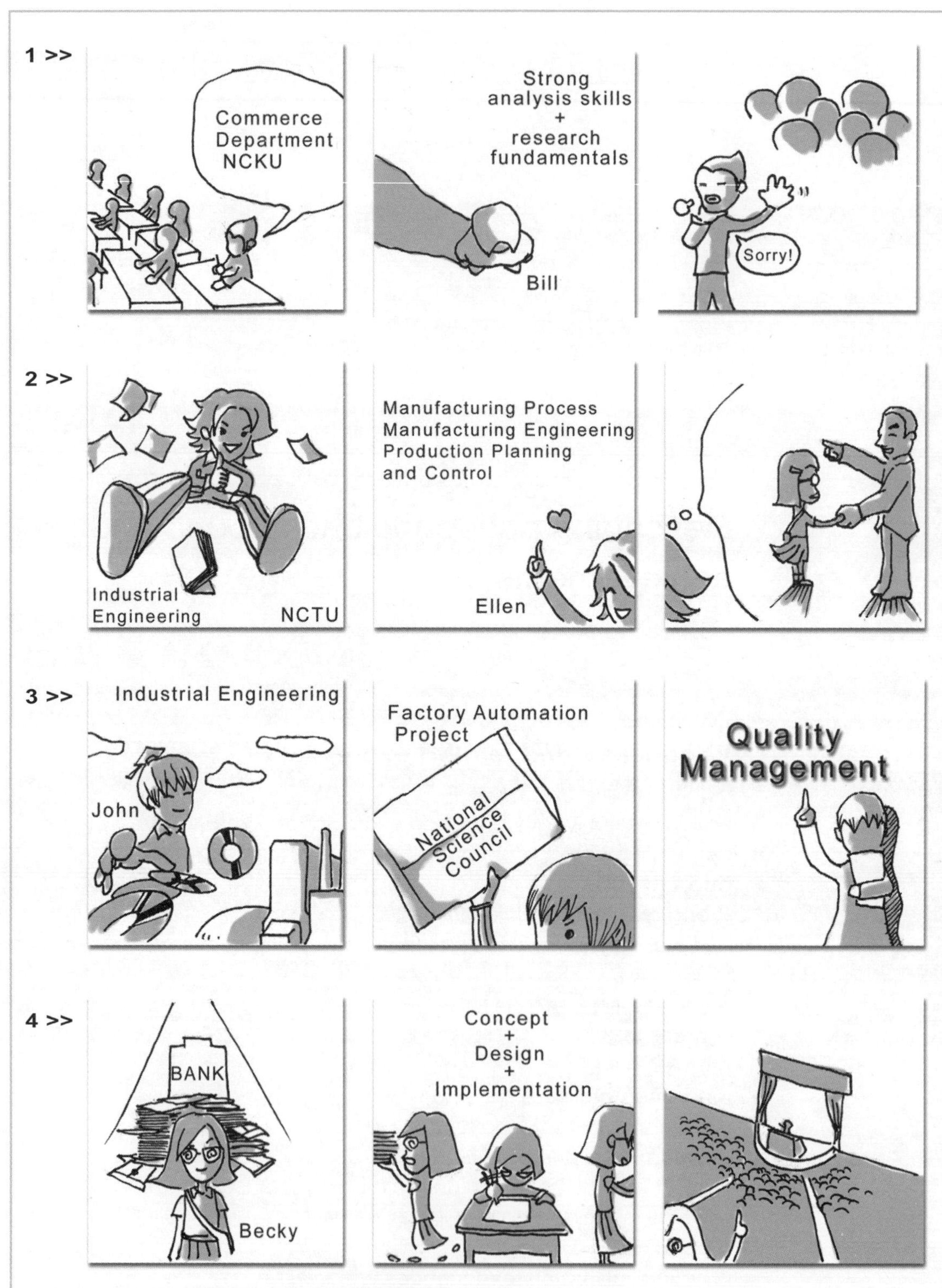

A **Write down the key points of the situations on the preceding page while the instructor reads the script on page 182 aloud.**

Situation 1

____

____

____

Situation 2

____

____

____

Situation 3

____

____

____

Situation 4

____

____

____

B **Based on the four situations in this unit, write three questions beginning with *Which* and answer them.**

Examples

Which department was Bill admitted to in 1999?
The Commerce Department at National Cheng Kung University.

Which university did John graduate from in 1999?
Feng Chia University

1. ______________________________

____

2. ______________________________

____

3. ______________________________

____

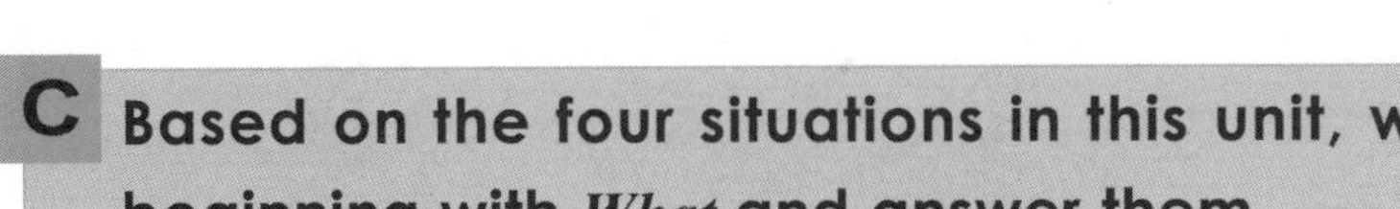

C **Based on the four situations in this unit, write three questions beginning with *What* and answer them.**

Examples

What fostered John's interest in factory automation in Taiwan?

Theoretical knowledge and practical laboratory experiences.

What type of National Science Council research project did Becky participate in during graduate school?

Projects that were related to deregulation of the banking industry in Taiwan and its financial impact.

1. ______________________________

____

2. ______________________________

____

3. ______________________________

____

D **Write questions that match the answers provided.**

Examples

What did Betty write that received considerable praise?

Her master's thesis

What gave John a further glimpse into the dynamic nature of industry-related research?

When he served as a teaching assistant for a quality management course

1. ______________________________

To conduct finance-related research

2. ______________________________

Yes.

3. ______________________________

To continue studies in Commerce

E **In the space provided, describe your academic background and achievements.**

____

____

____

____

____

____

Writing for Conciseness: Create Strong Verbs
(強有力的動詞)

As demonstrated in the previous unit, the action of a sentence can be stated more clearly when verbs are used rather than nouns. However, some verbs are weak in that they do not express a specific action. Verbs such as ***is, are, was, were, has, give, make, come*** and ***take*** are common examples. In contrast to using such weak verbs, a writer should employ strong verbs that imply a clear action. Consider the following examples:

如前單元所示，使用動詞使句子意念表現的更清晰，然而，有些動詞讓人感覺並不強勁，無法有力闡示一個動作。動詞如 **is, are, was, were, has, give, make, come,** 還有 **take** 等都屬此類。所以， 作者應使用強有力的動詞來指明一個清楚的行爲。細想以下例句：

Original
The student has the opportunity to attend numerous international conferences.
Revised
The student can attend numerous international conferences.

Original
Managers should make an attempt to clearly communicate their concerns.
Revised
Managers should attempt to clearly communicate their concerns.
Or more simply
Managers should communicate their concerns clearly.

Original
The students must offer a summary of their extracurricular activities.
Revised
The students must summarize their extracurricular activities.

F Correct the following sentences by using the copyediting marks on page 14.

1. No significant difference in test scores occurred between the two groups.

2. The gross domestic product was not significantly different between the two countries.

3. The performance is only a little affected by adjustment of the temperature.

4. An increase in government funding causes the student drop out rate to decrease.

5. The larger the university, the more diverse its student population.

6. The instructor placed an emphasis on how modern management practices are related.

7. First year graduate students must make an adjustment of their research interests according to their advisor's suggestions.

8. The committee members give a recommendation whether or not to accept the applicants.

9. Completion of the admissions process is required by all committee members so that objectivity can be ensured.

10. Acceptance to a particular graduate school program is heavily dependent on the candidate’s academic performance.

G Consider the following examples of how to describe your academic background and achievements:

My senior thesis on the synthesis of carbon nitride films to develop a novel bio-molecular organic vitamin enhanced my research and presentation skills. Following graduation, I pursued my research interests by submitting the findings of this thesis in a poster presentation at the Third Annual Organic Synthesis Symposium. From this experience, I not only learned the mechanics of writing a research paper, but also became aware of my lack of adequate knowledge in properly designing a study, evaluating data, and communicating my results orally. I believe that these skills are essential for researchers in this field. Therefore, I hope to refine these writing and presentation skills through the design of a similar work during graduate study.

~~~~~ * ~~~~~ * ~~~~~ * ~~~~~ * ~~~~~

During graduate school, I participated in several National Science Council research projects. These projects were related to deregulation of the banking industry in Taiwan as well as its subsequent financial impacts. Actively participating in each stage of the projects, from original concept formation and experimental process design to experimental implementation, not only improved my research skills but also broadened my knowledge base. Additionally, I attended many international conferences. These valuable experiences contributed significantly to my master's thesis, which
~~~~~

received considerable praise.

~~~~~ * ~~~~~ * ~~~~~ * ~~~~~ * ~~~~~

Graduate school enabled me to view engineering problems from an analytical perspective, as evidenced by my high academic standing. In my masters thesis entitled "Effective Control of a Structure's Shape Using Laminated Sensors and Actuators", I proposed a control algorithm that controlled a structure's shape without relying on external loading information. Portions of this thesis have been submitted for publication in the *Journal of Engineering Today* (A summary of the manuscript is enclosed.) Compiling the thesis exposed me to ongoing efforts to upgrade a tool machine's precision, which in turn increase the market competitiveness of locally manufactured products. Notably, when difficulties were encountered during my experiments, I was more so provoked to strive for successful results.

~~~~~ * ~~~~~ * ~~~~~ * ~~~~~ * ~~~~~

After passing a highly competitive nationwide university entrance examination, I was admitted to the Commerce Department at National Cheng Kung University in 1999 where I majored in Finance. Several academic awards, an overall academic ranking of first out of a class of 300 and a cumulative GPA of 3.95/4.0 attest to the strong analytical skills and research fundamentals that I developed in order to conduct finance-related research. Upon graduation, I refused several employment offers in the financial

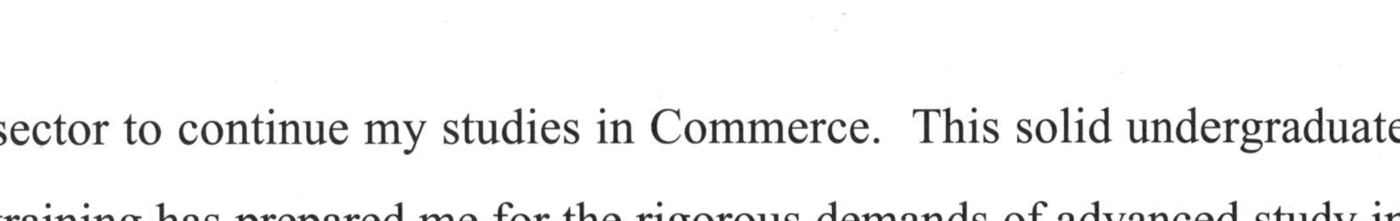

sector to continue my studies in Commerce. This solid undergraduate training has prepared me for the rigorous demands of advanced study in this field. After deliberate consideration, I am applying to your program.

* * * *

My scholastic achievement over the years has been very positive, with my grades steadily improving. My transcripts indicate that, as I became more comfortable and at ease with my new life as a college student, my grades improved each semester.

* * * *

Through my reading of numerous journal articles, I began to realize the dominating role that the United States plays in developing theories and applications. Thus, I have chosen to receive advanced training there.

* * * *

I graduated from the Industrial Engineering Department at Feng Chia University in 1999. The departmental curricula provided me with a theoretical and practical understanding of industrial occupations, particularly those in the electronics, telecommunications and semiconductor industries. Moreover, courses including Quality Control and Factory Automation were particularly effective in fostering my ability to solve problems logically.

* * * *

In addition, I served as a research assistant in a National Science Council sponsored project on factory automation in Taiwan. Although limited resources and facilities prevented me from an in depth investigation, theoretical knowledge and practical laboratory experiences furthered my interest in this field. I was also a teaching assistant for a course in quality management, which provided me with a more thorough understanding of the dynamic nature of industry-related research.

~~~~~ * ~~~~~ * ~~~~~ * ~~~~~ * ~~~~~

A sound academic background in Industrial Engineering at one of Taiwan's premier universities, National Chiao Tung University, has provided me with the fundamental skills required for advanced research. Courses of particular interest during university were Manufacturing Process, Manufacturing Engineering, Production Planning and Control, as well as Industrial Organization and Management. Coursework during both my junior and senior years heavily emphasized practical applications, often providing me with many opportunities to come to work with numerous enterprises.
~~~~~

Unit Four

Introducing research and professional experiences

介紹研究及工作經驗

Vocabulary and related expressions

a concentration in 主攻
premier 有名的
acquired 拿到
implement 執行
immersing 埋首於
administrative 行政的
recently emerging 新興的
intrigued 著迷
ensure 確定
distinguished 著名的
renowned 有名的
strong academic background 強有力的學歷背景
solid background 強有力的個人背景
rigorous challenges 嚴厲的挑戰

Unit Four Introducing research and professional experiences 介紹研究及工作經驗

A **Write down the key points to the situations on the preceding page while the instructor reads the script on page 188 aloud.**

Situation 1

____

____

____

Situation 2

____

____

____

Situation 3

____

____

____

Situation 4

____

____

____

B **Based on the four situations in this unit, write three questions beginning with *Where* and answer them.**

Examples

Where did John audit management courses?
The Institute of Technology Management at National Taiwan University.

Where did Julie study?
The Institute of Food Research at National Taiwan Normal University.

1. ______________________________

____

2. ______________________________

____

3. ______________________________

____

C Write three questions beginning with *What* and answer them.

Examples

What does Larry aspire to become?
A distinguished researcher.

What is Cathy's position at Chang Gung Memorial Hospital?
A physical therapist.

1. ______________________________

____

2. ______________________________

____

3. ______________________________

____

D Write questions that match the answers provided.

Examples

Where did John audit management courses?

National Taiwan University

When did Julie join the Food Safety Laboratory?

While working on her bachelor's degree

1. ______________________________

Personal intellect and determination

2. ______________________________

She can facilitate their improvement through therapy.

3. ______________________________

To understand how food poisoning affects humans

E In the space provided, state your research and professional experiences.

____

____

____

____

____

____

Writing for Conciseness: Avoid Overusing Sentences that Begin with *It* and *There*

避免過度使用 *It* 及 *There* 開頭句

Another form of wordiness and ambiguity is sentences beginning with ***There*** and ***It***.
使用 ***It*** 及 ***There*** 開頭的句子容易使文章語多累贅及曖昧不清。
Unless ***It*** refers to a specific noun in the previous sentence, omit ***It is*** entirely.

除非 ***It*** 指的是先前句子所提特定的名詞，否則完全的避免 ***It is*** 的句型。

Several common phrases beginning with ***It is*** can be omitted since they do not add to a sentence's meaning. Such examples include the following:
數個由 ***It is*** 開頭的句型應去除掉，因為他們對句意並沒幫助。諸如此類的例句尚包括：

It is well known that
It may be said that
It is a fact that
It is evident that
It has been found that
It has long been known that
It goes without saying that

If omitted entirely, several common phrases beginning with ***It*** and ***There*** can be stated more simply. Consider the following examples:
如果不能完全省略去除掉這種句型，則應更爲精簡地描述全句。細想以下例句：

Original
It is our opinion the assumption is true.
Revised
We believe the assumption is true.

Instead of	Say
Itispossiblethat	may, might, could
Thereis a need for	must, should
Itisimportantthat	must, should
It could happen that	may, might, could
There is a necessity for	must
It is necessary/critical/crucial/imperative that	must
Itisnotedthat	Notably,
It is interesting to note that	Interestingly,
Itisobvious/clearthat	Obviously,/ Clearly,

A simple way of omitting a phrase beginning with ***It is*** or ***There is*** is to delete ***that***, ***which***, or ***who*** behind the subject. Consider the following examples:
一個簡單去掉用 ***It is*** 或 ***There is*** 開頭句型的好方法是消除在主詞之後的 ***that***，***which*** ,或是 ***or*** 等字。細想以下例句：

Original
It is the student who spends much time preparing class assignments.
Revised
The student spends much time preparing class assignments.

Original
There are diverse educational practices that strengthen and broaden a student's knowledge base.
Revised
Diverse educational practices strengthen and broaden a student's knowledge base.

F Correct the following sentences by using the copyediting marks on page 14.

1. It is likely that the price of a private school education is higher than that of a public one.

2. There is a need to control the number of graduate students admitted each fall semester by the faculty committee.

3. It is essential that cooperation with each other is the goal of research team members.

4. It may happen that a decision to not attend a particular graduate school program is made by the applicant.

5. There is a necessity for an agreement on the research topic by the graduate school advisor and advisee.

6. It is critical that consideration of all available research programs is made by the graduate school applicant.

7. It is crucial that careful assessment of the candidate's academic potential is performed by the admissions committee.

8. It is not necessary for the presentation of a detailed research proposal be made by students in their graduate school application.

9. There is increasing evidence that suggests that there is a relation between academic performance and nutrition.

10. There is a limitation on the number of words in a Statement of Purpose for graduate study by many admissions committees.

G Consider the following examples on how to introduce one's research and professional experiences:

In addition to theoretical study at the masters level, I have emerged myself in hands-on experiences that fostered my creativity and enabled me to apply my academic knowledge to the semiconductor industry.

~~~~~ * ~~~~~ * ~~~~~ * ~~~~~ * ~~~~~

The project instilled in me the importance of collaborative teamwork and the ability to coordinate individuals in a group effort.

~~~~~ * ~~~~~ * ~~~~~ * ~~~~~ * ~~~~~

As an undergraduate student, I participated in technology management-related research, emphasizing the correlation between modern management practices. My findings culminated in publication of a research paper. To enhance my research abilities, I attended several international conferences and audited management courses at the Institute of Technology Management at National Taiwan University.

~~~~~ * ~~~~~ * ~~~~~ * ~~~~~ * ~~~~~

My studies at the Institute of Food Research at National Taiwan Normal University provided me with solid background knowledge of diet and nutrition, as well as the desire to become an academic researcher in this exciting field. While completing my Bachelor's degree, I joined the Food Safety Laboratory to understand the effects of food poisoning. This experience reinforced my dedication to laboratory work and stressed the
~~~~~

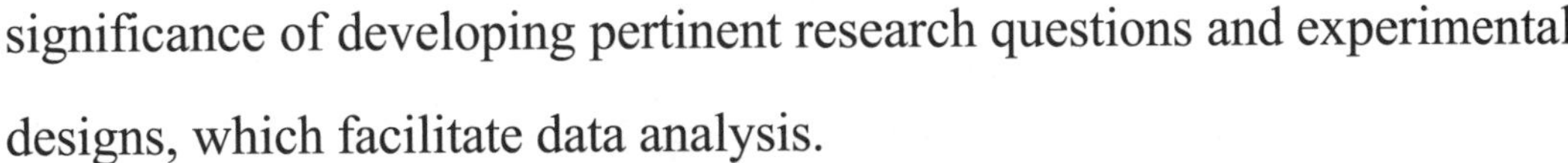

significance of developing pertinent research questions and experimental designs, which facilitate data analysis.

* * * *

In addition to my academic background, I have excelled in information technology-related skills, such as Photoshop, Powerbuilder Script, ASP, and Sybase Database. Continuously developing knowledge skills will largely determine my success as a computer programmer.

* * * *

In addition to nurturing my problem-solving skills and advanced knowledge in this field, the above experiences have sharpened my ability to define specific situations, think logically, collect related information, and analyze problems independently. These achievements reaffirm my determination to pursue further studies so that I will have studies, which will provide me with the necessary professional skills for my future career.

* * * *

During graduate study, I joined the Climatic Research Laboratory where I learned how to conduct independent research. My proposal to develop a climate model used in policy studies on global warming evidenced my ability to excel independently.

~~~~~ * ~~~~~ * ~~~~~ * ~~~~~ * ~~~~~

To supplement my current knowledge of psychology, I am currently enrolled in a Social Development course. Moreover, I participated in a research inquiry on the correlation between parental meta-emotion philosophy and attachment styles. I presented my findings at the Chinese Psychological and Behavioral Science Seminar held in December 2000. I thoroughly enjoy this research discipline, particularly the complete process of forming a construct, rendering a hypothesis, clarifying minute aspects and receiving critical comments from other researchers. I consider this more intriguing than simply obtaining anticipated results to validate an original hypothesis. Following undergraduate studies, I will continue to complete supervised research courses, which will nurture my research-related skills. This will be in addition to supplementing my studies with suggested readings regarding the welfare of young children. I believe that such preparation will enhance my future studies.

~~~~~ * ~~~~~ * ~~~~~ * ~~~~~ * ~~~~~

My current research project involves designing a questionnaire, interviewing participants and analyzing data. These experiences have exposed me to the dynamic structure of educational research and the exciting challenges of a research career. Although my aspiration of becoming a distinguished researcher will be arduous, I am prepared to immerse myself in Academia and believe that I have the intellect and determination to satisfy its challenges.

~~~~~ * ~~~~~ * ~~~~~ * ~~~~~ * ~~~~~

My work experience has enabled me to share my managerial experiences with classmates in the Graduate program as well as orient them on Taiwan's innovative managerial approaches. I am particularly interested in providing insight on the differences between Western and Asian managerial styles. I also believe that I can add to a class's diversity through my personal, educational and professional experiences while in turn offering a unique Asian perspective.

~~~~~ * ~~~~~ * ~~~~~ * ~~~~~ * ~~~~~

During summer vacations, I served as a research assistant in the Applied Environmental Sciences Laboratory, where I conducted preliminary experiments on dioxins and PCBs risk assessment. I also conducted independent research on the environmental impacts and risks of decommissioning oil platforms. This research strengthened my commitment to reducing environmental risks, which I intended to pursue during my doctoral studies at Michigan State University.

~~~~~ * ~~~~~ * ~~~~~ * ~~~~~ * ~~~~~

As a physical therapist at Chang Gung Memorial Hospital for the past five years, I find my work with physically challenged individuals personally fulfilling. I feel I can facilitate their improvement through therapy. In addition to providing therapy for children, I have gained advanced professional knowledge and, thus, believe that Graduate study would further
~~~~~

improve upon it. Moreover, I believe that a clinical practitioner examining therapeutic changes requires the skills to design and conduct a study, which your school will provide.

Unit Five

Describing extracurricular activities relevant to study

描述與學習有關的課外活動

Vocabulary and related expressions

equip 配備
exposure 暴露
peers 同伴
broaden one's horizons 擴展某人的視野
close collaboration 緊密的合作
coincide with 與　一致
unique leadership opportunity 獨特的領導機會
extracurricular activities 課外活動
necessary balance 必須的平衡
bilingual 雙語的
market niches 市場利基
the larger global picture 更寬大的國際視野
implementing 執行
sharpen one's negotiation skills 鋒利某人的談判技巧
the discrepancy between theory and practice 理論及實際上的差別
diverse education 不同的教育
enhance one's sensitivity 增加某人的感受
a turning point 轉捩點
coordinate 協調
applying knowledge skills 適用知識技巧
integrated and efficient manner 整合及有效率的方法
inspired 使有靈感

Unit Five Describing extracurricular activities relevant to study

描述與學習有關的課外活動

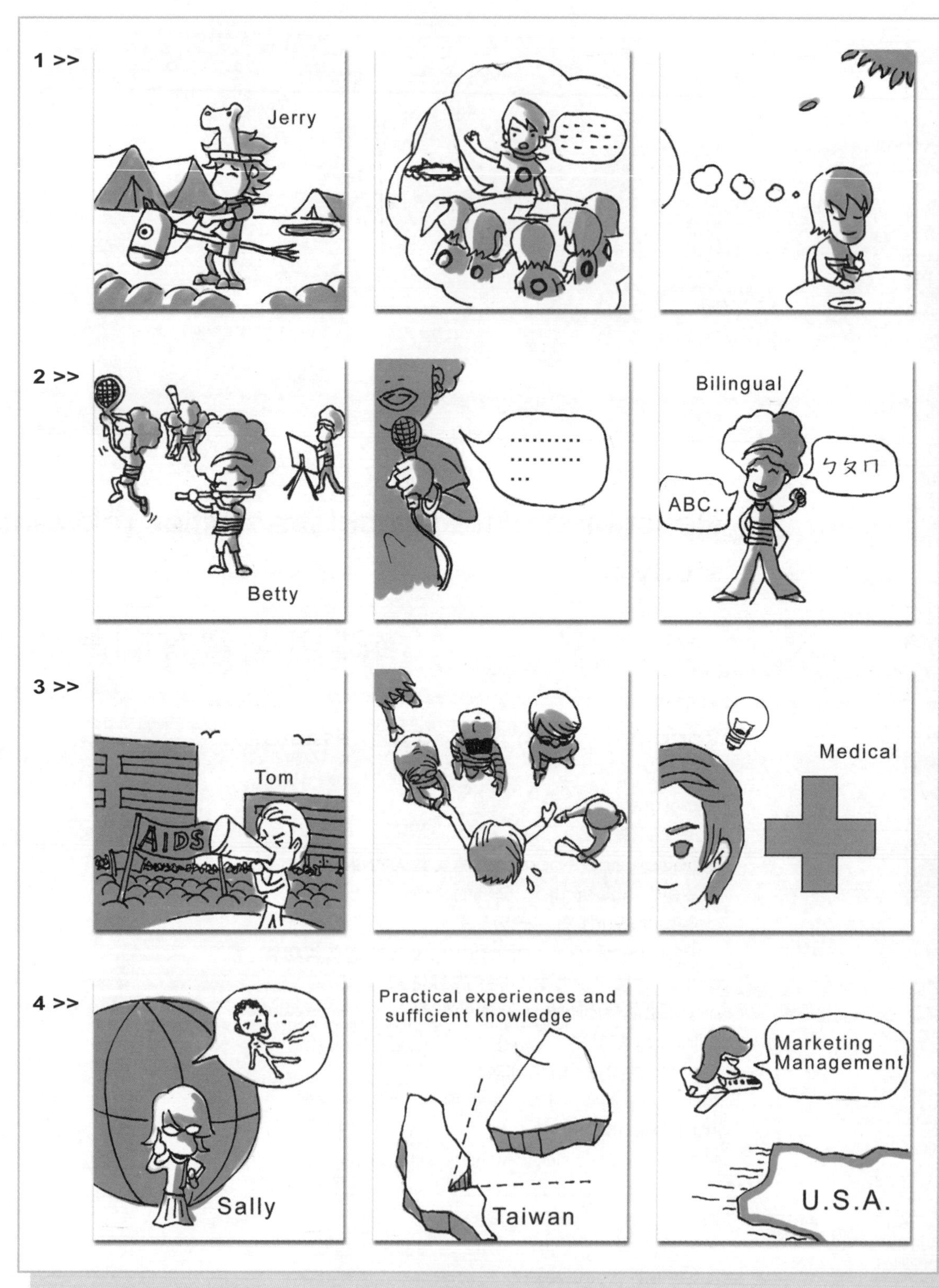

A **Write down the key points to the situations on the preceding page while the instructor reads the script on page 194 aloud.**

Situation 1

____

____

____

Situation 2

____

____

____

Situation 3

____

____

____

Situation 4

____

____

____

B **Based on the four situations in this unit, write three questions beginning with *Where* and answer them.**

Examples

Where does Sally hope to pursue an advanced degree in Marketing Management?

The United States.

Where did Jerry learn how to assume a leading role in planning programs?

A social service organization that hosted summer youth camps.

1. ______________________________

____

2. ______________________________

____

3. ______________________________

____

C **Based on the four situations in this unit, write three questions beginning with *What* and answer them.**

Examples

What type of campaign did Tom organize with other classmates?

AIDS awareness.

What did Betty participate in during university?

Many extracurricular activities.

1. ______________________________

____

2. ______________________________

____

3. ______________________________

____

D Write questions that match the answers provided.

Examples

How did Jerry attempt to keep volunteers at the youth camps involved?

Planning dinners that coincided with scheduling sessions, using a sensor of humor to retain everyone'sinterest, making related tasks enjoyable and, above all, providing an example of hard work for others to follow

Where has Sally decided to pursue an advanced Marketing degree?

The United States

1. ______________________________

She is bilingual.

2. ______________________________

She often served as a representative for or spokesperson of campus organizations.

3. ______________________________

He worked with other classmates in organizing an AIDS Awareness campaign on the university campus.

E In the space provided, describe extracurricular activities that are relevant to your field.

____

____

____

____

____

____

____

____

Writing for Conciseness: Delete Redundant and Needless Phrases
其他冗詞例句包括

Many statements of purpose are cluttered with redundant or needless phrases that can be either deleted entirely or expressed more simply.
The writer should try to avoid needless and redundant words and phrases, which only increase a sentence's length. Consider the following:

除去重複及不必要的措詞
這些擾人重複不必要的文詞其實可以完全去除，或是用更簡明的方式表達。作者若不注意這個細節則會使句子變得愈來愈長。細想以下例句：

Original
The doctoral candidate wants to take the opportunity to make an introduction of his research topic.
Revised
The doctoral candidate wants to introduce his research topic.

Other examples of wordy phrases include the following:

Wordy	Preferred
despite the fact that	although
be deficient of	lack
in a position to	can

Another form of redundancy is putting two words together that have the same meaning. Since "rule" implies something that is "general" the writer can easily cut this phrase in half by simply saying "rule" rather than "general rule". Other examples of such phrases that can be easily cut in half to simplify the meaning include

另一種重複語句是把 2 個具同樣意義的字放在一起。例如 rule 其實就包括 general 的意思，所以千萬不要寫出 general rule 這樣的文句，用 rule 來代表就可以了。其他的例句也如法炮製如下

Instead of	Simply say
true facts	facts
very unique	unique
rate of speed	speed
resemble in appearance	resemble
five in number	five
adequate enough	adequate (or enough)
close proximity	proximity
first priority	priority
definite decision	decision
future plans	plans
increase in increments	increase
future predictions	predictions
red colored	red
initial prototype	prototype
outside periphery	periphery
joint cooperation	cooperation
major breakthrough	breakthrough
most optimum	optimum
necessary requirement	requirement
cooperate together	cooperate

F Match the unclear word or phrase with the concise one. The first one has been completed.

Unclear	Concise
In many cases	never
in most cases	if
in no case	consider, examine
for this reason	exceeds
give consideration to	several, many
give indication of	if
happens to be	am/is/are
if conditions are such that	indicate/suggest
in a number of	to, for
in close proximity to	because, since
is in excess of	always
in large measure	so
in all cases	near
in case	thus, therefore
accordingly	largely
for the purpose of	often
for the reason that	usually

Match the unclear word or phrase with the concise one. The first one has been completed.

Unclear	Concise
reach a conclusion	after
serves the function of	how
subsequent to	ask about, inquire about
it is interesting that	conclude
it is our opinion that	although
manner in which	notably
notwithstanding the fact that	we believe
on the basis of	may, might, could, can
put an end to	is
the question as to	if
on the order of	about, approximately
prior to	from, because, by
provided that	whether
it is possible that	before
make inquiry regarding	interestingly
it is noted that	end

Match the unclear word or phrase with the concise one.
The first one has been completed.

Unclear	Concise
in the field of	so that
in the near future	to, for
in the neighborhood of	occasionally
is capable of	near
is found to be	in
is in a position to	if
in the event that	can
in order that	because, since
in order to	is
in some cases	soon
in the vicinity of	near, about, nearly
in this case	in
in view of the fact that	for
in terms of	here
in the amount of	for
in the case of	can

Match the unclear word or phrase with the concise one. The first one has been completed.

Unclear	Concise
by a factor of two	After
by means of	now
come to a conclusion	like
along the lines of	when
ascertain the location of	two times, double, twice
at this point in time	by
be deficient in	conclude
in a position to	because, since
at such time as	while
at the present time	now
despite the fact that	although
due to the fact that	most
during the time that	therefore
a majority of	find
accordingly	lack
after the conclusion of	can

G Consider the following examples of how to describe extracurricular activities that are relevant to study:

Collaborative experiences from extracurricular activities during my undergraduate degree have enabled me to effectively communicate with research associates that have diverse academic backgrounds.

~~~~~ * ~~~~~ * ~~~~~ * ~~~~~ * ~~~~~

In addition to the knowledge gained through coursework, I also collaborated with others in extracurricular activities, such as the debate club. In particular, during a summer camp, I lectured high school students on how to deliver an argument and persuade the audience effectively. I also ran the 300-meter dash on the university track team, which I received a gold medal during a regional meet. While the debate club supplemented my extracurricular knowledge, the track team nurtured my perseverance and endurance with its demanding practices.

~~~~~ * ~~~~~ * ~~~~~ * ~~~~~ * ~~~~~

In addition to studying diligently and maintaining a solid academic record, I have balanced my professional life with a diverse range of extracurricular activities. Participating in numerous activities has helped me nurture leadership and collaborative skills, which are essential to my future aims. Among the extracurricular activities I participated in at Chung-Hsing University was our Department's Student Association. In addition to its numerous academic activities, it also supplemented my knowledge of organizational operations as well as cultivated interpersonal and communication skills.

Unit Five Describing extracurricular activities relevant to study
描述與學習有關的課外活動

~~~~~ * ~~~~~ * ~~~~~ * ~~~~~ * ~~~~~

During university, I participated in a social service organization that hosted summer youth camps. After several years of participation, I gradually assumed a leading role in program planning for these camps. While providing sports, entertainment, and art-related activities, these camps equip students with communicative skills, provide exposure to peers and broaden their horizons.

~~~~~ * ~~~~~ * ~~~~~ * ~~~~~ * ~~~~~

Executing such a comprehensive camp schedule requires close collaboration among team members to ensure success. As a leader, I had to initiate innovative ways of maintaining volunteers. This included holding special dinners which coincided with planning sessions, using a sense of humor to retain everyone's interest, making related tasks enjoyable and, above all, providing an example of hard work. This unique leadership opportunity has been one of the most rewarding experiences of my undergraduate years.

~~~~~ * ~~~~~ * ~~~~~ * ~~~~~ * ~~~~~

Realizing that the medical profession should actively educate to avoid the spread of infectious diseases, I worked with other classmates in organizing an AIDS awareness campaign on the university campus. This campaign attempted to inform students of the devastating effects of this disease and illustrate numerous preventive measures. Implementing this project introduced me to various entities such as school administrators and
~~~~~

shop owners. As well, it sharpened my negotiation skills and showed me the discrepancy between theory and practice. This diverse experience strengthened and broadened my solid knowledge base, and further enhanced my sensitivity towards various medical issues.

~~~~~ * ~~~~~ * ~~~~~ * ~~~~~ * ~~~~~

I headed our department's student association during my junior year in university. In this capacity, I was responsible for holding academic workshops, managing departmental publications, and organizing social functions as well as other rewarding activities. These responsibilities allowed me to implement the organizational theories that I had learned in the classroom. Additionally, interacting with other project leaders strengthened my coordinating and leadership capabilities.

~~~~~ * ~~~~~ * ~~~~~ * ~~~~~ * ~~~~~

Serving as the public relations chairperson of a fundraising campaign for global hunger was a turning point in my decision to pursue a marketing career. I coordinated a large-scale marketing and promotion project for this challenging and worthwhile cause. While increasing my interest in communications, this experience also reaffirmed my ability to achieve my career goals by applying my knowledge skills systematically. Taiwan currently lacks individuals with both practical experience and sufficient knowledge to market products in an integrated and efficient manner. This demand has inspired me to pursue an advanced degree in Marketing Management in the United States.

Unit Five Describing extracurricular activities relevant to study
描述與學習有關的課外活動

~~~~~ * ~~~~~ * ~~~~~ * ~~~~~ * ~~~~~

During my undergraduate studies, I joined a university-sponsored activity, working with mentally and physically challenged children. The children were unique in their unique life experiences. For example, some parents may have placed unrealistic expectations on their healthy child, while others may have neglected them because as they had to spend more time with their challenged one. I remember once during a game of making wishes, a little boy wished that his little sister would be as healthy as he was. Unexpectedly, the children who were listening suddenly began to cry. Such a public expression of intense emotions reaffirmed the reasons why I chose this line of work. I am also a volunteer with the Mental Retardation Foundation. I am appalled at the lack of an inclusionary education program for challenged children. Therefore, I am excited by your Psychological Studies in Education program.

~~~~~ * ~~~~~ * ~~~~~ * ~~~~~ * ~~~~~

The numerous extracurricular activities that I participated in during university gave me the necessary balance of developing academic and social skills simultaneously. I often served as a representative or spokesperson of campus organizations, subsequently making many new friends and building my self-confidence. In addition to a solid academic background, as a skilled manager I have strong communicative, organizational and management skills. Also, the fact that I am bilingual allows me to adjust easily to foreign cultures and understand how different market niches apply to the larger global picture.

Unit Six

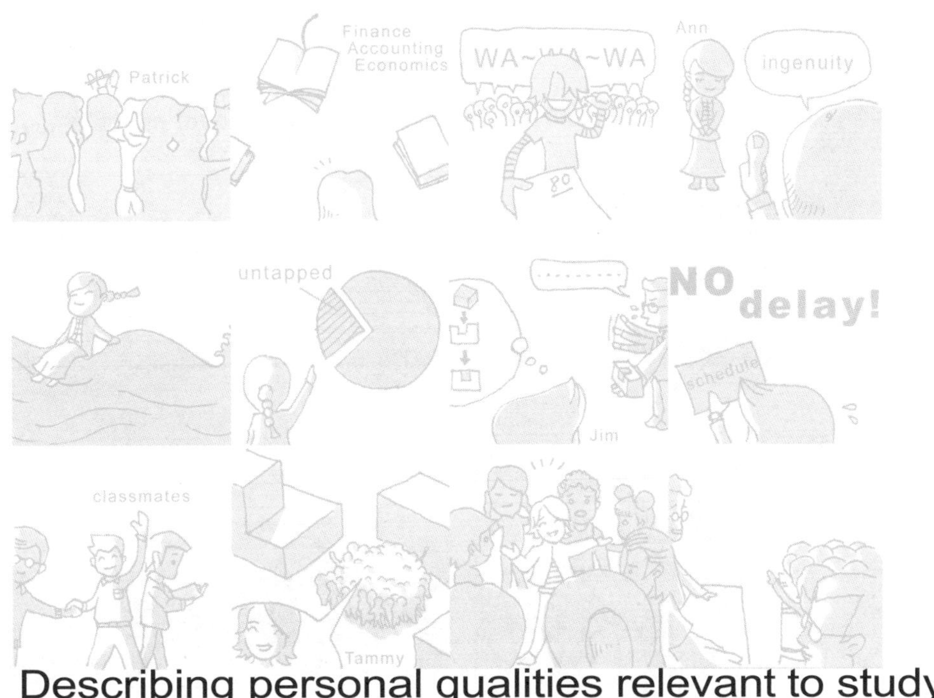

Describing personal qualities relevant to study

描述與學習有關的個人特質

Vocabulary and related expressions

Undistinguished academic work 混亂的學業成績
grade point average 平均成績
desire to be a high achiever 高成就慾望
ingenuity 獨創性
inherited 傳承
nurtured 教養
in tune with popular trends 清楚知道流行趨勢
a passing fad 一時的風尚
an emerging trend 新興趨勢
remain abreast 朝同一方向並列
attest to 證明
quickly generate 快速產生
closely monitor 緊密監控
incur 招致
efficiently resolve 有效地解決
positively contribute to 明確地貢獻
nurtured 培養
collaborate with 和...合作
interact with 互相影響

1 >>
Patrick
Finance
Accounting
Economics
WA~WA~WA
80
2 >>
Ann
ingenuity
untapped
3 >>
Jim
NO delay!
schedule
classmates
4 >>
Tammy

A Write down the key points to the situations on the preceding page while the instructor reads the script on page 200 aloud.

Situation 1

____

____

____

Situation 2

____

____

____

Situation 3

____

____

____

Situation 4

____

____

____

B **Based on the four situations in this unit, write three questions beginning with *What* and answer them.**

Examples

What were Patrick's final course grades during his last two years of university?

80 or higher.

What allowed Tammy to assess different situations rationally in both of her jobs?

Communication skills.

1. ______________________________

____

2. ______________________________

____

3. ______________________________

____

C **Write three questions whose answers begin with *Yes* or *No* based on the four situations in this unit and answer them.**

Examples

Does Tammy believe that graduate school will provide her with many opportunities to collaborate and interact with classmates?

Yes, she does.

Is Jim worried about his performance in graduate school?

No, He is confident that he can contribute positively to collaborative efforts by classmates.

1. ____________________

2. ____________________

3. ____________________

D Write questions that match the answers provided.

Examples

What kind of person is Tammy?

She is friendly and communicative.

What can Ann often pinpoint?

The untapped market demand of a certain group

1. ______________________________

A passing marketing fad and an emerging trend

2. ______________________________

Creativity

3. ______________________________

Superiors, clients, agents, speakers, scholars and experts

E **In the space below, describe your personal qualities that are relevant to study.**

____

____

____

____

____

____

Writing for clarity: Ensure subject and verb agreement

單元二 ： 主詞及動詞必須前後呼應

Subject and verb disagreement confuses a reader. Furthermore, it creates confusion regarding how many people, places or objects are involved, and also creates a faulty logic. A primary reason for subject-verb disagreement is a failure to recognize them accurately.

如果主詞的單複數與動詞不能配合，不僅讀者感到困惑，同時句子的邏輯也會發生問題。

1. The number of applicants applying to graduate school are increasing.

   The number of applicants applying to graduate school is increasing.

   The subject must agree with the verb. *The number of* **takes a singular verb while** *A number of* **takes a plural verb.**

2. The majority of the admissions committee feel that the most qualified candidates were selected.

The majority of the admissions committee feels that the most qualified candidates were selected.

The verb should be singular since the noun committee refers to *a unit* of people. However, consider the following sentence:

The majority of graduate school applicants have strong analytical skills.

In this case, the verb should be plural since the noun refers to *individual* applicants.

3. Patience as well as honesty are important during the application procedure.

Patience as well as honesty is important during the application procedure.

Expressions such as *as well as, in addition to, along with, accompanied by* and *with* should not confuse the reader into thinking that the sentence has a compound subject and, therefore, should have a plural verb.

4. Either the number of applicants or available vacancies determines the outcome of the committee's decision.

Either the number of applicants or available vacancies determine the outcome of the committee's decision.

Whenever *or* or *nor* connects two subjects, the subject closest to the verb should decide whether the verb is singular or plural. Since *vacancies* is the closest to the verb, the verb should be plural.

5. The laboratory head and professor are my graduate advisor.

   The laboratory head and professor is my graduate advisor.

   Or

   The professor who acts as the laboratory head is my graduate advisor.

   Although a plural verb is normally used when two or more subjects are connected by *and*, a singular verb should be used when the two or more subjects refer to the same person or thing.

6. Economics have become an increasingly popular graduate program in recent years.

   Economics has become an increasingly popular graduate program in recent years.

   If a noun is plural in form (ending in "s" or "es"), this does automatically imply that it is plural in meaning. Like *economics*, other examples such as *mathematics*, *physics* and *telecommunications* take singular verbs because they refer to a single body of knowledge.

7. Everyone are planning to attend the college fair.

   Everyone is planning to attend the college fair.

   Although pronouns like *everyone* or *everybody* may imply more than one person, the writer should not mistakenly choose a plural verb. Singular verbs should be used for the following pronouns: *anybody, anyone, each, either, every, everybody, everyone, neither, nobody, no one, one, somebody, someone,* and *something.*

8. The introductory course in research orientation that was designed to train First-year graduate students are open for enrollment.

   The simulation program that was designed to identify consumer tastes is ready for implementation.

   Writers should be careful not to choose the wrong verb form by becoming distracted by words or phrases between the subject and the verb.

9. *Dumb and Dumber* continue to be a widely watched comedy among video renters.

   Dumb and Dumber continues to be a widely watched comedy among video renters.

   Even if the subject is plural in form, names of companies, and titles of books or plays require a singular verb.

F Correct the following senentences by circling the singular or plural form of the verb.

1. A number of graduate schools (has, have) offered writing courses for first-year graduate students who are non-native English speakers.

2. A graduate school applicant that (chooses, choose) to provide ample information that is relevant to his or her academic background (allows, allow) the admissions committee to more easily evaluate the potential of that individual to fulfill course requirements.

3. Determination along with intelligence significantly (affects, affect) a graduate student's academic performance.

4. Neither extracurricular activities nor academic background solely (determines, determine) acceptance to graduate school.

5. To express interest in a field of study and display current knowledge of that field (is, are) essential for an effective study plan.

6. Telecommunications (is , are) a newly emerging field in Taiwan's industrial sector.

7. Each of the points in this book (contributes , contribute) to a successful study plan.

8. The procedure which students (follows , follow) to gain admittance to graduate school (requires , require) much patience.

9. Outlining one's career objectives in addition to stating why a particular institution is selected for advanced study (plays , play) an important part of one's study plan.

10. The number of admissions committees that require a study plan (has, have) increased in recent years.

G Consider the following examples on how to describe personal qualities relevant to study :

Another one of my strong personality traits is personal determination to achieve goals (academic or otherwise).

~~~~~ * ~~~~~ * ~~~~~ * ~~~~~ * ~~~~~

My previous academic performance and related experiences reflect my strong determination to pursue an advance degree in communications engineering.

~~~~~ * ~~~~~ * ~~~~~ * ~~~~~ * ~~~~~

I am friendly and communicative. While in university, I participated in the student government association in our department. During that period, I had many opportunities to interact with individuals from diverse backgrounds and could easily accommodate myself within a group. In both of my jobs, I had to communicate frequently with employers, clients, agents, speakers, scholars and experts. Communication skills were nurtured, allowing me to assess different situations rationally. Graduate school will provide me with many opportunities to collaborate and interact with classmates and professors, as well as occasionally meeting with entrepreneurs. These are situations in which I am highly competent.

~~~~~ * ~~~~~ * ~~~~~ * ~~~~~ * ~~~~~

Despite the occasional frustrations of daily life, I have maintained an optimistic attitude as reflected by my personal ambition to pursue a research career in Academia.

~~~~~ * ~~~~~ * ~~~~~ * ~~~~~ * ~~~~~

I view disappointments and trials as an opportunity to learn and, thus, strengthen my personal stamina.

~~~~~ * ~~~~~ * ~~~~~ * ~~~~~ * ~~~~~

In sum, I am creative, responsible and friendly. While some individuals consider expertise as the most essential quality, I feel that a congenial, yet strong-willed personality creates happiness and success. Therefore, I believe
~~~~~

my personality will add greatly to graduate studies, both for myself and for my classmates.

~~~~~ * ~~~~~ * ~~~~~ * ~~~~~ * ~~~~~

My employers have often commented on my ingenuity when confronted with complex situations. While some asserted that this is inherited, creativity can be nurtured through training. For example, I am familiar with popular trends and can often distinguish between a passing fad and an emerging trend. By remaining abreast of consumer behavior within a target group, I can often pinpoint the untapped market demand of a certain group.

~~~~~ * ~~~~~ * ~~~~~ * ~~~~~ * ~~~~~

My colleagues and superiors can attest to my responsible and trustworthy character. When assigned a task, I quickly generate a schedule, draft the details and closely monitor it through to completion. I strongly believe that planning is essential to successfully coordinating tasks and achieving goals. When unforeseen obstacles may arise and cause a delay, I ensure efficient resolution. I will apply this same responsible attitude to graduate study as well as any research effort. Furthermore, I am confident that I can contribute positively to collaborative efforts in graduate school.

~~~~~ * ~~~~~ * ~~~~~ * ~~~~~ * ~~~~~
~~~~~

My academic performance during university is a notable example of my diligence. Despite my undistinguished academic work during the first two years of university, I was determined to raise my grade point average. However, I did not flinch from taking rigorous courses such as Finance, Accounting and Economics. Moreover, in the courses that I completed during my last two years of university, I received grades of 80 or higher. In addition to coursework, my personal actions reflect my goal-oriented nature.

Unit Seven

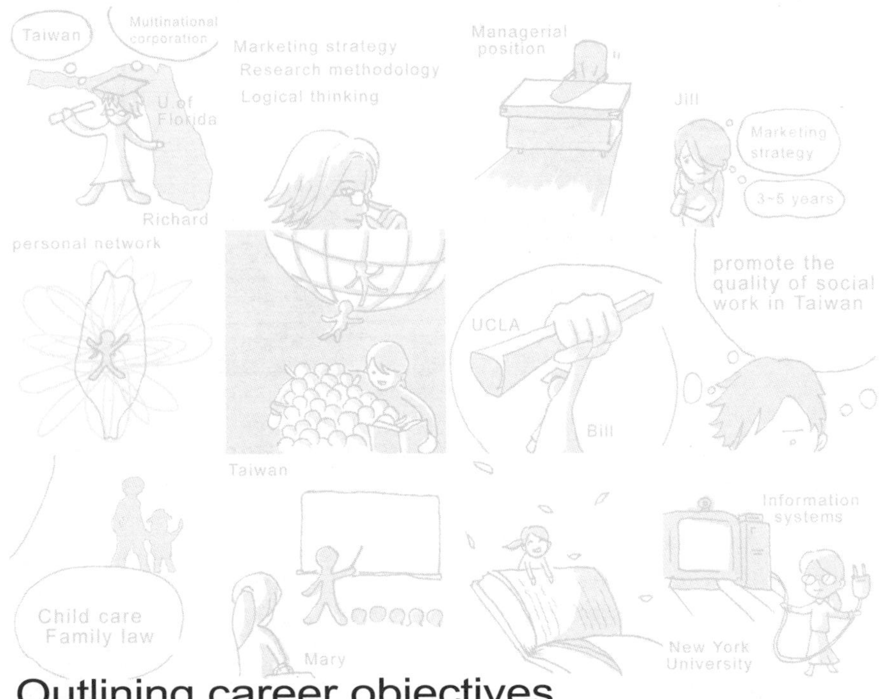

Outlining career objectives

概述未來工作目標

Vocabulary and related expressions

logical thinking 合理的思考
latest technological advances 最新的科技
exposure to 暴露於
receptive 善於接受的
place one in line for 把某人置於和...同一方向
export 輸出
emerging markets 新興市場
to be in a better position to 位於較有利地位
equipped 配備

1 >>
Taiwan
Multinational corporation
U.of Florida
Richard
Marketing strategy
Research methodology
Logical thinking
Managerial position
2 >>
Jill
Marketing strategy
3~5 years
personal network
3 >>
UCLA
Bill
promote the quality of social work in Taiwan
Child care
Family law
4 >>
Taiwan
Mary
Information systems
New York University

A **Write down the key points to the situations on the preceding page while the instructor reads the script on page 204 aloud.**

Situation 1

____

____

____

Situation 2

____

____

____

Situation 3

____

____

____

Situation 4

____

____

____

B **Based on the four situations in this unit, write three questions beginning with *Why* and answer them.**

Examples

Why does Bill want to eventually earn a doctorate degree in social work?

To be in a better position to promote the quality of social work in Taiwan.

Why does Jill want to teach marketing theory?

So that more people can contribute to Taiwan's competitiveness in global markets.

1. ______________________________

____

2. ______________________________

____

3. ______________________________

____

C Write four questions beginning with *What* and answer them.

Examples

What does Jill want to do after successfully completing MIT's academic requirements?

To work for roughly three to five years as a marketing strategist.

What is Bill especially interested in?

Child care and family law.

1. ______________________________

____

2. ______________________________

____

3. ______________________________

____

D **Write questions that match the answers provided.**

Examples

What does Jill plan to teach someday?

Marketing theory

How long does Jill plan to work as a marketing strategist?

Roughly three to five years

1. ______________________________

The graduate program at New York University

2. ______________________________

Improving and revising software processes

3. ______________________________

Case studies as well as statistical and theoretical analysis

E In the space provided, describe your career objectives.

____

____

____

____

____

____

Writing for clarity: Ensure that pronoun references are clear in meaning
（單元三 ： 代名詞必須清楚的使用）

Readers become confused when sentences contain pronouns that do not have a clear antecedent. An antecedent is what a pronoun refers to. Numerous problems can arise when a pronoun does not refer to a clear antecedent. For instance, a pronoun can refer to more than one antecedent.
如果代名詞所指的人物或事物不能交待清楚，也是徒增讀者困惑。
For instance, a pronoun can refer to more than one antecedent. Consider the following example:

The interviewer told the applicant that she had to leave the meeting early.

In the sentence, confusion over who **she** refers to, the **interviewer** or the **applicant**, makes the reader wonder who must leave the classroom early. If **she** refers to the **student**, then the sentence's intended meaning can be expressed as

The interviewer told the applicant, "You must leave the meeting early."
OR
The interviewer told the applicant to leave the meeting early.

Another problem is that placing the pronoun far away from its antecedent makes it more difficult for the reader to understand what the pronoun refers to. Consider the following example:

The chef slowly poured the spaghetti sauce into the pan and waited until the temperature reached the boiling point; it lasted for five minutes.

In the sentence, what the antecedent refers to is difficult to determine since it is far removed from its antecedent. Clearly stating what it refers to omits confusion and, therefore, the revised sentence is as follows:

The chef slowly poured the spaghetti sauce into the pan and waited until the temperature reached the boiling point; the procedure lasted for five minutes.

Yet, confusion is also caused by improper use of antecedents that involves using **which**, **this**, and **that** when referring to a previous clause within a sentence. Consider the following:

The procedure requires several minutes, which complicates the overall process.

In the sentence, **which** may create confusion over what the writer is referring to. The following revisions can omit this potential confusion:

The procedure requires several minutes, thereby complicating the overall process.
OR
The procedure, requiring several minutes, complicates the overall process.
OR
The fact that the procedure requires several minutes complicates the overall process.
OR
The procedure requires several minutes; this time period complicates the overall process.

F Correct the following sentences by using the copyediting marks on page 14.

1. It is the responsibility of the committee chairman to supervise all admissions procedures.

2. It is well known that preparing a rough draft of a study plan allows applicants to present their ideas more thoroughly.

3. The admissions process takes a considerable amount of time, which implies that all submitted materials are carefully reviewed.

4. In a study plan, it is expected that applicants describe the motivation for pursuing an advanced degree.

5. In Taiwan's telecommunications industry, they are applying advanced technologies because the Island has a globally competitive export market.

6. They stated in their report how admissions procedures should be changed.

7. When admissions committees apply different standards to select candidates, they have difficulty in achieving a uniform criteria.

8. They demonstrated in an earlier investigation that graduate school applicants tend to reveal personal qualities that reflect academic potential for advanced study.

9. It is widely recognized that the accounting program at Indiana University ranks consistently high in national surveys.

10. It is the assumption of the admissions committee that all submitted materials are original.

G Consider the following examples on how to outline career objectives:

I have decided to devote my career to researching Taiwanese art history. Despite the obvious lack of a research discipline in this area, I believe that I can contribute to preserving Taiwanese art for future generations.

~~~~~ * ~~~~~ * ~~~~~ * ~~~~~ * ~~~~~

After completing a masters degree in Strategic Management from the University of Florida, I will return to Taiwan prepared to make a significant contribution. I plan to work in a multinational corporation or research institute. Marketing strategy, research methodology and logical thinking - all of which nurtured in the masters program - will enable me to respond effectively to the latest technological advances in the workplace. As well, my exposure to case studies as well as statistical and theoretical analysis will render me more receptive to novel concepts. Combining work experiences with a master's degree, I hope to eventually attain a managerial position.

~~~~~ * ~~~~~ * ~~~~~ * ~~~~~ * ~~~~~

Despite my solid academic training, I still feel somewhat unprepared for the workplace, particularly a research position in Academia. Therefore, during my MS program, I would be quite interested in learning more about research methods, statistics and advanced financial theories. Such foundational courses would place me in a strong position to eventually pursue a Ph. D in Marketing or Management.

~~~~~ * ~~~~~ * ~~~~~ * ~~~~~ * ~~~~~

Upon completion of my graduate degree, I hope to return to Taiwan and acquire a teaching position in a junior college or university. By acquiring advanced knowledge and specialized skills that your program offers, I will be well equipped and more confident to manage such a position. As well, my experiences gained through your graduate program will also contribute to the development of information systems in Taiwan, which has recently began to focus on improving and reusing software processes.

~~~~~ * ~~~~~ * ~~~~~ * ~~~~~ * ~~~~~

Owing to the current shortage of professional expertise in Internet marketing in Taiwan, after completing my master's degree, I plan to return to Taiwan and work with an Internet advertising agency. I am convinced that the professional training from your university will provide me with numerous opportunities to put my knowledge and skills to deserving use.

~~~~~ * ~~~~~ * ~~~~~ * ~~~~~ * ~~~~~

Following successful completion of your program's requirements, I plan to work roughly three to five years as a marketing strategist, preferably analyzing potential markets to enhance export growth. This work will hopefully enable me to more thoroughly understand emerging markets in Taiwan and to establish an extensive personal network that facilitates further research. Beyond that initial five-year time frame, I hope to contribute to
~~~~~

my country through aiding the Government in constructing sounder strategic policies. I also plan to teach marketing theory, which will enable more people to contribute to Taiwan's competitiveness in global marketplace.

~~~~~ * ~~~~~ * ~~~~~ * ~~~~~ * ~~~~~

After successfully completing a master's degree from your university, I plan to continue onto a doctoral degree. This would place me to be in a better position to promote marketing strategy in Taiwan.

~~~~~ * ~~~~~ * ~~~~~ * ~~~~~ * ~~~~~

As a short term goal, I would like to become a high-level manager, drawing on my marketing educational, professional and field experiences to execute sound management decisions. In addition to applying theory to the workplace, I hope to teach strategic management on the university level to foster interest in this exciting field.

~~~~~ * ~~~~~ * ~~~~~ * ~~~~~ * ~~~~~

In the long term, I plan to eventually pursue a Ph.D. in a related field. A masters degree as well as work and teaching experiences will provide the foundation for a subsequent level of study. I am interested in researching strategic management topics at either a university or research institute. Following doctoral studies, I plan to be a university professor while serving as a management consultant for companies attempting to determine their niche in the global marketplace.

~~~~~ * ~~~~~ * ~~~~~ * ~~~~~ * ~~~~~

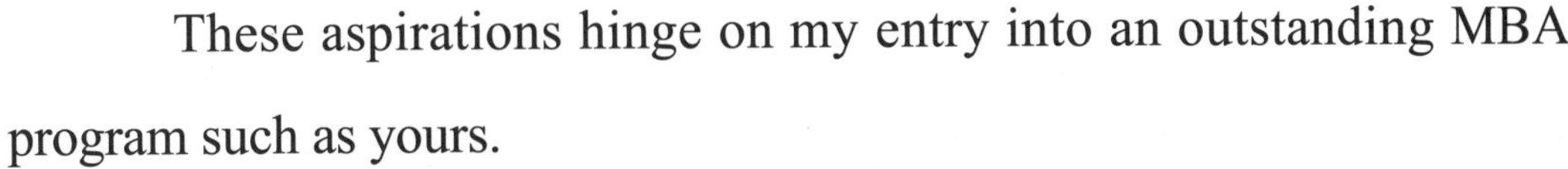

These aspirations hinge on my entry into an outstanding MBA program such as yours.

* * * *

Although I am not exactly certain of my field of study, I am highly interested in food research and its relation to nutrition. After fulfilling my doctoral requirements, I will return to Taiwan where I hope to work in a research institute and develop organically healthy foods. Owing to the lack of nutritionists in Taiwan that concentrate on synthetic food development, I would like to fill in that gap by establishing more effective and successful measures to promote the local food industry.

* * * *

After completing a graduate degree program, I will apply this professional knowledge to a career in the information industry or with government. I believe that completing the Computer Science graduate program at Columbia University is the only way to fully realize my career aspirations.

* * * *

After completing a doctoral program, I will contribute to my country through researching new financial theories and aiding the Government in constructing sounder financial markets. Via a teaching position, I will share financial and economic theories so that more people might contribute further to outstanding financial management in Taiwan.

~~~~~ * ~~~~~ * ~~~~~ * ~~~~~ * ~~~~~

Owing to my deep-rooted interest in this area, I have always aspired to excel as a human resources manager. I have actively prepared for a career in this field by closely scrutinizing my previous experiences, particularly those related to my diverse education of recent years. In addition to the Management course at National Chung Hsing University, I completed courses in organizational behavior, organizational psychology, and human resource administration at Tung Hai University. These institutions provided me with the fundamentals deemed essential for advanced study.

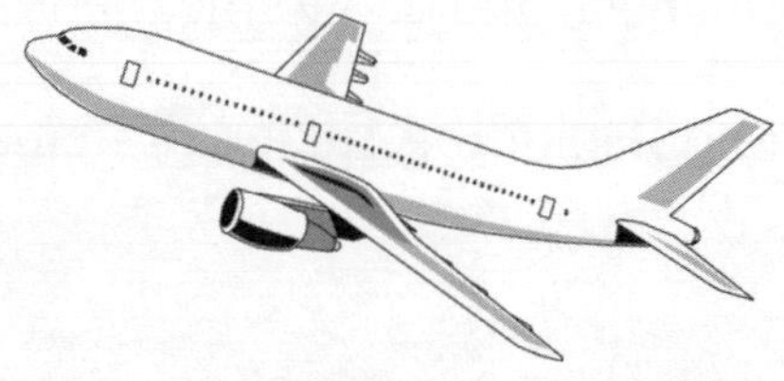
~~~~~

Unit Eight

Stating why an institution was selected for advanced study

解釋選擇該校原由

Vocabulary and related expressions

career aspiration 職業抱負
enhance 提高
foster 培育
aspiration 抱負
logical next step 合理的下一步
solid 強有力的
graduate curricula program 研究所課程
seemingly unlimited 似乎是無限制的
academic resources 學業資源
distinct 區別
unique 獨特的
diverse and professional curricula 互異及專業的課程
equip 配備
competence 勝任
flexibility 適應性
insight 洞察力
rich pool of talented individuals 有天份的個人
thrive 繁榮
as evidenced by 證明
relatively unscathed 相對地未受損失的
vibrant 振動的
dominant 佔優勢的
related theories and applications 相關的理論及應用

Unit Eight Stating why an institution was selected for advanced study

解釋選擇該校原由

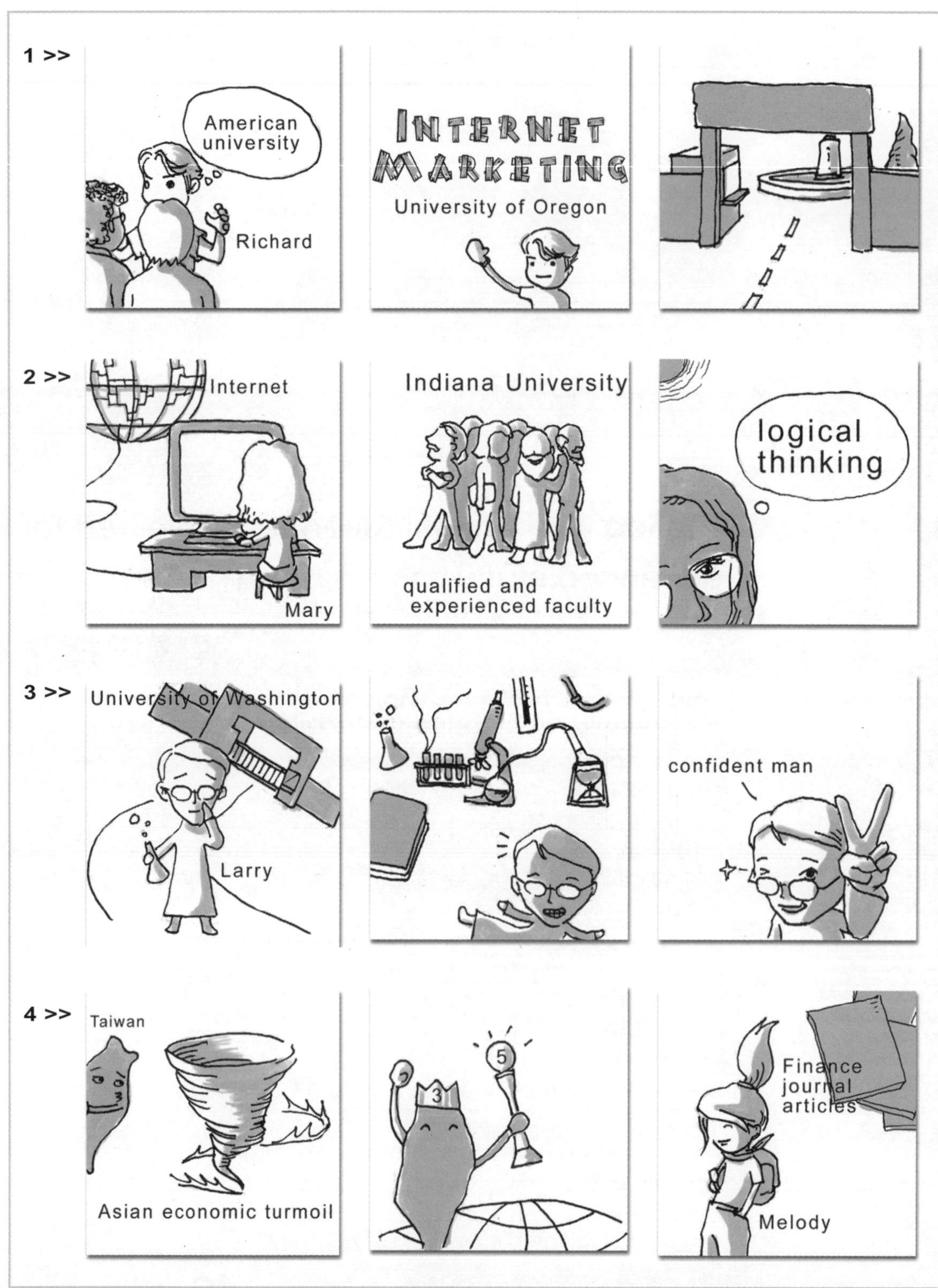

A **Write down the key points to the situations on the preceding page while the instructor reads the script on page 210 aloud.**

Situation 1

____

____

____

Situation 2

____

____

____

Situation 3

____

____

____

Situation 4

____

____

____

B **Based on the four situations in this unit, write three questions beginning with *Where* and answer them.**

Examples

Where did Mary begin searching for a graduate school through which she can achieve her goals?

The Internet, periodicals, and magazines.

Where would Richard like to attend graduate school?

The University of Oregon.

1. ______________________________

____

2. ______________________________

____

3. ______________________________

____

C **Based on the four situations in this unit, write three questions beginning with *What*.**

Examples

What country plays a dominant role in developing financial theories and applications?

The United States.

What does the Chemical Engineering Department at the University of Washington focus on?

Equipping its graduates with the technical competence and flexibility necessary to respond effectively to challenges within the Chemical engineering profession.

1. ______________________________

____

2. ______________________________

____

3. ______________________________

____

D Write questions that match the answers provided.

Examples

Does Mary believe that logical thinking is essential to professionalism in accounting?

Yes, she does.

What about the University of Washington is Larry the most attracted to?

Its diverse and proffessional curricula

1. ______________________________

Graduate study

2. ______________________________

Its weather and geographical conditions

3. ______________________________

A solid background in Chemistry

E In the space below, state why you have selected a particular institution for advanced study.

____

____

____

____

____

____

Writing for Clarity: Form sentences parallel in structure and meaning)
（ 單元四 ： 句子的結構須有一致性 ）

Parallelism in technical writing implies that all parts of a sentence must have a similar construction .
科技英文寫作中，句子的建構必須有一致性。
Consider the following example of a sentence that is not parallel:

The graduate program will enable Tom to improve his research skills and he can publish his findings in international journals.

Herein, putting the first part in active voice and the second part in passive one creates an unbalanced sentence. The revision should read as follows:

The graduate program will enable Tom to improve his research skills and to publish his findings in international journals.

Consider another example of a sentence that is not parallel in structure:

Professors must either assume sole responsibility for the success of a project or authority must be delegated to research assistants.

In this sentence, the correlative expression of **either...or** does not have a parallel structure. The revised sentence should read as follows:

Professors must either assume sole responsibility for the success of a project or delegate authority to research assistants.

Yet another example of this parallel problem is

Success in graduate school depends on the following:

Preparing for class assignments,
Consulting the teacher during office hours,
All textbook materials must be thoroughly read,
Getting at least seven hours of sleep daily, and
All appointments must be kept.

Sentences containing lists must also be parallel in structure. The revised sentence should read as follows:

Success in graduate school depends on the following:

Preparing for class assignments,
Consulting the teacher during office hours,
Thoroughly reading all textbook materials,
Getting at least seven hours of sleep daily, and
Keeping all appointments.

F Correct the following sentences by using the copyediting marks on page 14.

1. The study plan is promising, creative, and the author writes well.

2. The committee made a decision to accept six candidates and that the meeting should be adjourned.

3. Graduate students select a research topic under the guidance of their advisors and deadlines are set to monitor progress of the thesis.

4. Writing an effective study plan consists of the following:

Expressing interest in a field of study,

Displaying current knowledge of that field,

Academic background and achievements are described,

Research and professional experiences are introduced,

Describing extracurricular activities relevant to study, and

Relevant personal qualities to study are described.

5. Most study plans neither require a detailed outline for the thesis nor must a literature review be provided.

6. The study plan should outline career objectives and explaining the reason for selecting that institution.

7. The study plan should also describe extracurricular activities that are relevant to study and that research and professional experiences are introduced as well.

8. The previous approach is complicated, inefficient and wastes too much time.

9. Effective study plans include a description of an applicant's academic background and achievements as well as expressing interest in a field of study.

10. The applicant focused on an introduction of her research and professional experiences and to display current knowledge of her field of interest.

G Consider the following examples on how to state why an institution was selected for a particular field of study:

Earning a graduate degree from your prestigious institution would fully prepare me for a career in the semiconductor industry. Furthermore, I believe that graduate education in the United States would fully equip me with the latest skills required to thrive in this highly competitive field.

~~~~~ * ~~~~~ * ~~~~~ * ~~~~~ * ~~~~~

Fully aware of the graduate curricula and academic expectations at the University of Florida, I feel that this institution is the best place to fully realize my goals. I am confident that my firm commitment to receiving a graduate degree in social work will help me satisfy the rigorous requirements of your institution.

~~~~~ * ~~~~~ * ~~~~~ * ~~~~~ * ~~~~~

Your university's excellent academic and clinical environment will allow me to achieve the goals I have created for myself.

~~~~~ * ~~~~~ * ~~~~~ * ~~~~~ * ~~~~~

To achieve the above aspirations, applying to your prestigious Department of Chemical Engineering is the logical choice for me. The diverse and professional curriculum is what attracts me the most to the University of Washington. I am particularly drawn to your programs that focus on equipping its graduates with the technical competence and flexibility necessary to respond effectively to challenges within that
~~~~~

profession. I believe that I have the talent, insight, intelligence, creativity, and potential to contribute to the rich pool of talented individuals at your university. With a solid background in Chemistry along with my strong interests in the field, I am confident that I can contribute significantly to any research team that I belong to.

~~~~~ * ~~~~~ * ~~~~~ * ~~~~~ * ~~~~~

I began searching for a graduate school from which I hope to achieve my career goals. Via the Internet, periodicals and magazines in our university library, I discovered that the accounting program at Indiana University, a graduate school that has consistently ranked highly in national surveys, meets my requirements. What attracted me most was the highly qualified and experienced faculty with frequent publications in prestigious journals, seemingly unlimited academic resources, as well as its distinctive and unique tradition. I believe that logical thinking is essential to professionalism in accounting and your program would provide me with the knowledge required to achieve my ambitions. In addition, the weather and geographical conditions are agreeable to me.

~~~~~ * ~~~~~ * ~~~~~ * ~~~~~ * ~~~~~

I chose Belgium for my graduate studies to more thoroughly understand the European Union Market, which is largely misunderstood in Taiwan. Once I have firmly grasped how the EU market functions, I can apply my already thorough understanding of East Asian markets to attain a more global marketing perspective. While undergraduate courses in Strategic Management, Global Economics and Marketing provided solid fundamentals, I would like to expand on those core courses by concentrating on International Finance.

~~~~~ * ~~~~~ * ~~~~~ * ~~~~~ * ~~~~~

With its renowned global reputation, I am confident that Northwestern University can provide me with the skills necessary to thrive in the financial sector.

~~~~~ * ~~~~~ * ~~~~~ * ~~~~~ * ~~~~~

Graduate study in the United States would equip me with the skills necessary to thrive in the workplace. Evidenced by rapid industrial expansion and market deregulation, Taiwan's economy has flourished in recent decades. Although the island passed through the Asian economic turmoil of the late 1990s relatively unscathed, its revenues generated from information products and its average stock trading volume rank third and fifth worldwide, respectively. Growing up in such an economically dynamic environment has motivated my interest to research how domestic companies can compete with multinational corporations and how our government can adjust financial market strategies to enhance local competitiveness. My review of numerous journal articles has led me to understand the dominant role that the United States plays in developing related theories and applications.

~~~~~ * ~~~~~ * ~~~~~ * ~~~~~ * ~~~~~

To achieve my career aspirations, I intend to enhance my education through a graduate degree program at an American university. From various conversations, I have concluded that graduate study in the United States is the most effective means for me to achieve the training that I will require as the future leader in the organization in which I am currently employed. Admissions to the MA degree program in Internet Marketing at the University of Oregon will foster the skills I need to fully realize my aspiration of becoming an information specialist in the marketing field. Graduate study is the logical next step to fully realizing my career potential. The solid graduate curricula program at your university will build upon and refine the fundamental skills that I gained during undergraduate study.

~~~~~ * ~~~~~ * ~~~~~ * ~~~~~ * ~~~~~

I decided to go abroad for graduate school not only to expand my understanding of economics, but also to gain invaluable experiences that will benefit my future work and enrich my life.

~~~~~ * ~~~~~ * ~~~~~ * ~~~~~ * ~~~~~

The Indiana University Graduate program in Applied Chemistry will provide me with integrated courses as well as well-equipped laboratories and resources. Furthermore, this excellent academic program and clinical environment will allow me to eventually pursue a career as a chemist. The fieldwork course that includes professional knowledge of applied chemistry
~~~~~

will enable me to hone my laboratory techniques. Moreover, these course contents will assist me in related future employment. That is, this program will provide me with the skills required to become a highly qualified chemist in Taiwan.

Unit Nine

Recommending a student for study(Part A):

Introduction and qualification to make recommendation

撰寫推薦信函（A 部份）

推薦信函開始及推薦人的資格

Vocabulary and related expressions

exemplary academic performance 示範的學業表現
provide valuable insight into 提供寶貴的眼光
as documented in 以前曾提及
play an instrumental role in 扮演關鍵的角色
aptly convey one's confidence in 適當地表現某人的自信
enrolled 註册
enthusiastically contributed to 熱情地貢獻
inspiring other students to 激勵其他學生去
exceed one's expectations 超過某人的預期

Unit Nine Recommending a student for study (Part A): Introduction and qualification to make recommendation

撰寫推薦信函(A 部份)推薦信函開始及推薦人的資格

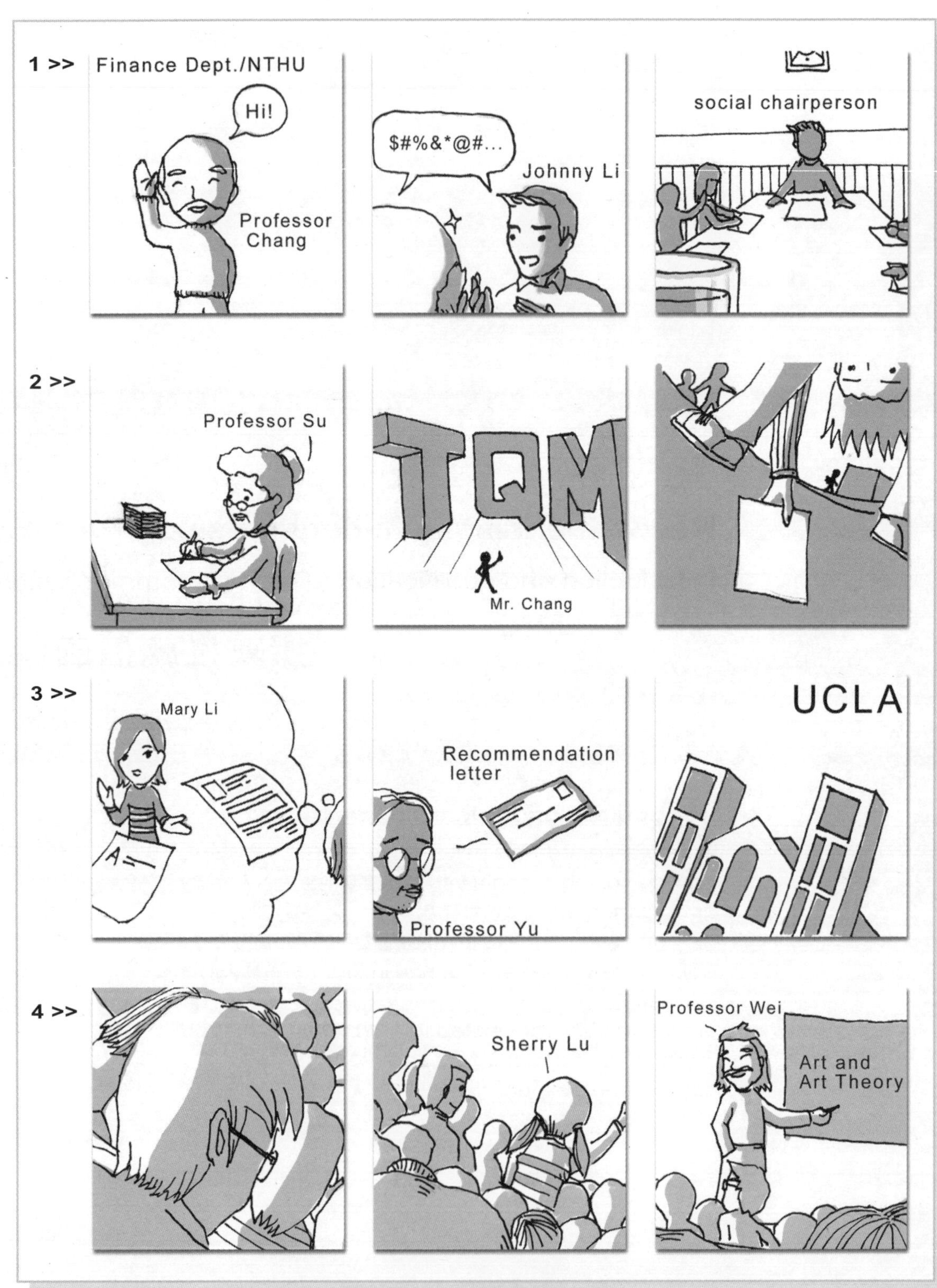

A Write down the key points to the situations on the preceding page while the instructor reads the script on page 216 aloud.

Situation 1

____

____

____

Situation 2

____

____

____

Situation 3

____

____

____

Situation 4

____

____

____

B **Based on the four situations in this unit, write three questions, which are answered by either *Yes* or *No* and answer them.**

Examples

Is Professor Chang the chairperson of the Ecology Department at National Tsing Hua University?

No, He is chairperson of the Finance Department at National Tsing Hua University.

Is Professor Yu recommending Mary Li for admissions to UCLA's master's degree program in Strategic Management?

Yes, he is.

1. ______________________________

____

2. ______________________________

____

3. ______________________________

____

C Write four questions that begin with *What* and answer them.

Examples

What position did Johnny Li hold in the department's student association?

Social chairperson.

What course did Mary Li enroll in during her junior year of university?

Advanced Accounting.

1. ____

   ____

2. ____

   ____

3. ____

   ____

D Write questions that match the answers provided.

Examples

What course did Professor Chang teach that Johnny Li enrolled in?

Global Economics

What university offers a Master's degree in Strategic Management?

UCLA

1. ______________________________

Yes

2. ______________________________

During her junior year

3. ______________________________

She inspired other students to participate more actively.

E **In the space below, recommend a student for advanced study via an introduction and also state your qualification to make such a recommendation.**

____

____

____

____

____

____

Eliminate modifier problems

單元五 ： 去除修飾語所造成的問題

As a word, phrase, or clause, a modifier describes another word, phrase, or clause. The reader becomes confused when the modifying clause or phrase is not adjacent to the word it modifies. This often creates a gap between the author's intended meaning and what is actually written.

修飾語必須放在所要修飾的字之旁。

Consider the following examples:

To write an effective study plan, preparation of all documents must be made by applicants.

Logically, **preparation** can not **write an effective study plan**. Therefore, placing the modifying clause next to what it modifies and through switching from passive to active voice makes the intended meaning clear:

To write an effective study plan, applicants must prepare all documents.

Placing the subject towards the front of the sentence clarifies the intended meaning:

Applicants must prepare all documents to write an effective study plan.

Consider another example of a modifier-related problem:

As a graduate student, my advisor taught me how to perform statistical analysis.

Similar to the above example, **a graduate student** mistakenly implies the subject of the sentence, which is **my advisor**. The revision should read as follows:

My advisor taught me how to perform statistical analysis when I was a graduate student.

A dangling modifier lacks the proper word in a sentence to modify, thereby making the sentence illogical. Consider the following example:

Original
Being a complex problem, the computer programmer derived the equation with much precision.

Revised
Because the equation contained a complex formula, the computer programmer derived it with much precision.

F Correct the following sentences by using the copyediting marks on page 14.

1. To express interest in a particular field, a related background is strongly advised for an applicant.

2. Before submitting a study plan, the institution must be selected.

3. When writing a study plan, personal qualities that reflect academic potential should be highlighted.

4. When describing extracurricular activities, their relevance to graduate study must be pointed out.

5. A study plan written by an applicant which was well structured was warmly received.

6. When stating why an institution was selected for advanced study, its reputation in a particular field should be mentioned.

7. Before recommending a student for a graduate program, personal details of the applicant should be obtained.

8. To outline one's career objectives in a study plan, a long-term goal should be highlighted.

9. Having a large database, the latest information on Graduate programs in France can be located in the campus network.

G Consider the following examples on how to make an introduction and state your qualification to make a recommendation:

His articulate speaking skills and logical train of thought struck me immediately. He briefly reviewed his undergraduate research through a professional slide presentation that immediately drew a positive response from the admissions committee. He later requested that I serve as his advisor, to which, I agreed without hesitation.

~~~~~ * ~~~~~ * ~~~~~ * ~~~~~ * ~~~~~

I am pleased to recommend Ms. Becky Chang, a highly ambitious individual, for admission to your rigorous Electronics Engineering program.

~~~~~ * ~~~~~ * ~~~~~ * ~~~~~ * ~~~~~

As chairperson of the Technical Management program at Soochow University and a frequent reader of management reports, I must often indicate errors in undergraduate work and comment on their overall quality. At the beginning of the semester, I often criticized the work of Mr. Jerry Chang's team in my Total Quality Management course. However, his team gradually advanced in its preparation and overall quality of work. In doing so, they provided valuable insight into how total quality management has been increasingly adopted in Taiwan's semiconductor industry, as documented in a report they wrote to fulfill the course requirements. Mr. Chang played a leadership role in this team, not only in orally presenting group findings but also in assigning work to team members.

~~~~~ * ~~~~~ * ~~~~~ * ~~~~~ * ~~~~~

As department chairperson of Applied Chemistry at National Taiwan Ocean University, I feel that I am in a good position to evaluate the preparedness of Ms. Jenny Su for graduate study in the same field at your institution.
~~~~~

~~~~~ * ~~~~~ * ~~~~~ * ~~~~~ * ~~~~~

Mr. Jang completed several courses that I taught, such as Marketing, Finance, and Economics.

~~~~~ * ~~~~~ * ~~~~~ * ~~~~~ * ~~~~~

Enrolled in three of my courses, Ms. Chuang enthusiastically contributed to my class, subsequently inspiring other students to participate more actively. In addition, her excellent academic performance exceeded my expectations that are based on many years of teaching.

~~~~~ * ~~~~~ * ~~~~~ * ~~~~~ * ~~~~~

I hope that this letter aptly conveys my confidence in Ms. Mary Li's ability to not only to meet the academic requirements but to excel in your Master's degree program in Strategic Management. In addition to observing her academic performance while enrolled in my Advanced Accounting course during her junior year, I have also been able to monitor her work performance in my accounting lab over the past six months.

~~~~~ * ~~~~~ * ~~~~~ * ~~~~~ * ~~~~~

As Chairperson of the Finance Department at National Tsing Hua University, I had the opportunity to closely observe Mr. Johnny Li when he completed my Global Economics course. In addition to his exemplary academic performance, Mr. Li also served as an officer of the department's student association.

Unit Ten

Recommending a student for study(Part B): Personal qualities of the candidate that are relevant to Graduate Study

撰寫推薦信函（ B 部份）

被推薦人與進階學習有關的個人特質及信函結尾

Vocabulary and related expressions

frequently engaging others in discussion 頻繁地和他人討論
persistent 堅持的
merit 優點
invaluable 無法估價的
hesitate 猶豫
diligent 勤奮
encounter a bottleneck 遭遇瓶頸
to delve into 鑽研
on one's own initiative 某人的主動行動，倡議
relevant 有關的
synthesize 合成
pertinent 恰當的
logical next step 合理的下一步
hypothesis 假說
asset 資產
innovative 創新的
carefully thought out 小心地仔細考慮
to be impressed with 對某人有很深的印象
highly qualified candidate 高度合格候選人

Unit Ten Recommending a student for study (Part B): Personal qualities of the candidate that are relevant to Graduate Study

撰寫推薦信函(B 部份)被推薦人與進階學習有關的個人特質及信函結尾

A **Write down the key points to the situations on the preceding page while the instructor loud the script on page 220 aloud.**

Situation 1

____

____

____

Situation 2

____

____

____

Situation 3

____

____

____

Situation 4

____

____

____

B Based on the four situations in this unit, write three questions beginning with *What* and answer them.

Examples

What never ceases to amaze Professor Chang?

Susan's diligent attitude towards studying.

What unique ability does Tom have?

The unique ability to identify exactly what he lacks for a particular research objective.

1. ____

2. ____

3. ____

C Write four questions beginning with *Why* and answer them.

Examples

Why is Susan applying to MIT's graduate program?

To undertake innovative research in chemical engineering.

Why is Professor Li qualified to recommend John Wang for graduate study?

John often served as a team leader in his research group.

1. ______________________________

____

2. ______________________________

____

3. ______________________________

____

D Write questions that match the answers provided.

Examples

Why will Susan be a great asset to any future research effort that she belongs to?

Her creativity and cooperative nature

What did the weekly group meetings that Betty participated in involve?

Journal discussions and case reports

1. ______________________________

____

A strong personality and effective communication skills

2. ______________________________

____

Reading

3. ______________________________

____

Five years

E **In the space below, recommend a student for advanced study by describing the personal qualities that are relevant to graduate study and conclude the letter with a closing statement or summary.**

____

____

____

____

____

____

Verify for faulty comparisons and omissions
再次檢查錯誤的比較詞及粗心的疏漏

Sentences that contain comparisons, which are illogical and incomplete create further ambiguity in writing. Editors must also recognize words that have been omitted carelessly.
不合邏輯及不完整的比較詞造成更多的含糊不清，同時注意不小心漏掉的字。

Consider the following examples:
The traditional approach performs less efficiently.
In the sentence, **The traditional approach performs less efficiently than** what?

For clarity, the revised sentence should read as follows:
The traditional approach performs less efficiently than the proposed one.

Or consider another example of a faulty comparison:
The students respect the teacher more than the graduate assistant.

Depending the author's intended meaning, the revised sentence should read as follows:
The students respect the teacher more than they respect the graduate student.
OR
The students prefer the teacher more than the graduate student does.

Consider two more examples:

Original
The application procedures are as complicated, if not more complicated than, the old ones.

Revised
The application procedures are as complicated as, if not more complicated than the old ones.

Original
Applicants should attempt describe their academic bacround and achievements as concisely as possible.

Revised
Applicants should attempt to describe their academic bacround and achievements as concisely as possible.

F Correct the following sentences by using the copyediting marks on page 14.

1. Her study plan is more thorough with respect to knowledge of the field of study.

2. The Chemistry Department comes into contact with school administration more than other departments.

3. The candidate's professional experiences are as in depth, if not more so than, other applicants.

4. The Chemistry Department's publications in international journals are more than the French Department.

5. Sue has always been fascinated the way in which successful managers can think creatively when making decisions.

6. Our proposal has a higher likelihood of success.

7. The graduate school emphasizes journal publications more than the undergraduate one.

8. The acceptance rate at Jones University is as high, if not higher than, other public institutions.

9. Jerry is interested studying organizational design.

10. Thompson University's dropout rate is lower than St. Mary's University.

G Consider the following examples on how to recommend a student for advanced study by describing the personal qualities that are relevant to graduate study and concluding the letter with a closing statement or summary:

Over the past two years that I have known her, I am most impressed by Ms. Wang's energy, as evidenced by her impressive class performance as well as the high esteem that her classmates and professors hold for her. Her enthusiasm in fully grasping concepts related to ethnomusicology impressed me deeply. If her four years of hard work and perseverance at our Music Department is any indication, I am confident that she will be able to meet the rigorous requirements of your school's graduate curricula.

~~~~~ * ~~~~~ * ~~~~~ * ~~~~~ * ~~~~~

Following graduation, Miss Li has continued to pursue her academic interests actively. For instance, in addition to teaching computers at a senior high school, she is simultaneously completing courses in advanced
~~~~~

programming and computer languages at National Chiao Tung University.

~~~~~ * ~~~~~ * ~~~~~ * ~~~~~ * ~~~~~

In light of her ability to quickly grasp abstract concepts, creativity, as well as her personal initiative, and willingness to accept others' constructive criticism, I highly recommend her for admission to your Doctoral program in Computer Science. Do not hesitate to contact me if I can provide you with any further insight into this highly qualified candidate.

~~~~~ * ~~~~~ * ~~~~~ * ~~~~~ * ~~~~~

As a student, she worked diligently to further develop her naturally gifted talent and displayed a seemingly boundless amount of energy while under my instruction. I was particularly struck by her total commitment to archeology. Her intelligence, industriousness, and dedication to this field will undoubtedly benefit her advanced studies. I do not hesitate in giving Ms. Chen my highest recommendation to pursue advanced study abroad.

~~~~~ * ~~~~~ * ~~~~~ * ~~~~~ * ~~~~~

Armed with a passion for archeology, Mr. Li assisted the department in conducting numerous excavations during his undergraduate years. His maturity and diligence help him focus on particular goals and provide him with the means to achieve them. This is evident in his demonstrated analytical skills and sound ability to formulate opinions after synthesizing available knowledge. Undoubtedly, these capabilities significantly contributed to his academic achievements, but will also ensure his future
~~~~~

success in Archeology. I fully endorse Mr. Li in his desire to pursue graduate study in this exciting field. Please do not hesitate to contact me if you have further questions regarding this highly qualified candidate.

~~~~~ * ~~~~~ * ~~~~~ * ~~~~~ * ~~~~~

I hold no reservations in recommending this highly qualified candidate for admissions to your Graduate program.

~~~~~ * ~~~~~ * ~~~~~ * ~~~~~ * ~~~~~

Her diligent attitude towards studying never ceased to amaze me. For instance, whenever encountering a research bottleneck, she consistently delved into reading and investigating the source of the problem while consulting with me on how to resolve the problem. Since graduation, she continues to maintain contact with several researchers in the field, discussing issues related to their clinical or research experiences. In addition, her critical thinking skills are remarkable, as evidenced by her ability to synthesize pertinent reading materials, identify limitations of previous literature and then state the logical next step from a unique perspective. Moreover, her analytical skills are exemplary. Although occasionally unfamiliar with the research topic at the outset, she analyzed the most pertinent information within her field of interest and then identified the research questions and hypothesis.

~~~~~ * ~~~~~ * ~~~~~ * ~~~~~ * ~~~~~

Her creativity and cooperative nature will be a great asset to any future
~~~~~

research effort that she belongs to. The opportunity to pursue advanced study in your graduate program will prepare her for further innovative research. I, therefore, have no hesitations in highly recommending this candidate for admission into your graduate program.

~~~~~ * ~~~~~ * ~~~~~ * ~~~~~ * ~~~~~

She constantly reviews related theory and discusses her observations with classmates. During our weekly group meetings, which involved journal discussions and case reports, she actively participated through her carefully composed questions and responses to other participants' views.

~~~~~ * ~~~~~ * ~~~~~ * ~~~~~ * ~~~~~

In addition to her strong academic performance, I was also impressed with her optimism. For instance, in addition to seeking me out on Finance-related matters, she also sought out experts in the field to discuss their experiences. Such enthusiasm displays her determination to purse a career in Finance. I hold no reservations in recommending this highly qualified candidate for admissions to your Graduate program.

~~~~~ * ~~~~~ * ~~~~~ * ~~~~~ * ~~~~~

Academically, Mr. Lu is a highly motivated student who never missed a class and actively participated in class discussions and assignments.

~~~~~ * ~~~~~ * ~~~~~ * ~~~~~ * ~~~~~

During her senior seminar courses, she undertook a pilot study to fulfill his thesis requirement. Upon graduation, she presented portions of that thesis in a poster presentation at an international symposium. During this period, she often queried me on how to plan and write a research paper, which is quite a daunting task for an undergraduate student. I am quite confident of her ability to complete graduate studies and believe that she will greatly contribute to any research team.

~~~~~ * ~~~~~ * ~~~~~ * ~~~~~ * ~~~~~

Based on my observations, I have no qualms in recommending this highly qualified candidate for admission to your graduate program.

~~~~~ * ~~~~~ * ~~~~~ * ~~~~~ * ~~~~~

Mr. Li has an outgoing personality, as evidenced by his leadership role in student government. His assumed responsibilities and high degree of efficiency gained the praise of his classmates. Furthermore, his refined coordinating skills and direct communication facilitated the smooth running of events and policies. Thus, his strong leadership potential will prove to be a valuable asset for any research team that he belongs to.

~~~~~ * ~~~~~ * ~~~~~ * ~~~~~ * ~~~~~

Professionally, Mr. Wang has proven himself to be one of the best swimming instructors in our fitness center, as reflected by the responsible and efficient manner in which he conducts himself as an extremely patient teacher of novice swimmers. He interacts well with the children and their parents often comment on his reliability. Having expressed a strong desire to develop his interest in physical education, he often consults me on how
~~~~~

to encourage the children to improve their performance. Moreover, his enthusiasm for sharing new information with others has gained the respect of his colleagues. I have no hesitations in recommending this worthy candidate for admissions to your prestigious graduate program. Please contact me if I can provide any further insight into Mr. Wang's ability.

~~~~~ * ~~~~~ * ~~~~~ * ~~~~~ * ~~~~~

John often served as a team leader in my research group, frequently engaging other team members in discussion and assigning tasks. I largely attribute the team's excellent performance to his persistent direction. Importantly, he appears to have learned the merit of listening carefully to others opinions, even when his views differ.

~~~~~ * ~~~~~ * ~~~~~ * ~~~~~ * ~~~~~

I cannot emphasize enough my confidence in Mr. Wang's ability and determination to successfully complete his graduate studies. In addition to his academic potential, a strong personality and superior communication skills will prove invaluable for the challenges of graduate study. The admissions committee is welcome to contact me for further insight into this highly qualified candidate.

~~~~~ * ~~~~~ * ~~~~~ * ~~~~~ * ~~~~~

Mr. Su has been an associate scientist at our laboratory for five years. He is responsible for performing various experimental procedures and analyzing the results. His diligence in collecting and organizing materials
~~~~~

within the laboratory has played an important role in our product development efforts. He has the unique ability to identify exactly what is required for a particular research objective. He also quickly understands the limitations of conventional research. Moreover, he has undertaken experiments enthusiastically, attempting to solve problems from various angles. Remaining confident despite occasional setbacks, Mr. Su remained perseverant during experimental work, ultimately resulting in the establishment of a standardized laboratory process.

~~~~~ * ~~~~~ * ~~~~~ * ~~~~~ * ~~~~~

Furthermore, he has the keen ability to address problems effectively, as evidenced by his exemplary presentation and organizational skills during weekly meetings. That is, his presentations were professionally delivered and well prepared.

~~~~~ * ~~~~~ * ~~~~~ * ~~~~~ * ~~~~~

With his vast laboratory experience, insight, and positive attitude towards eliminating ambiguity in environmental waste programs, I am highly confident of Mr. Su's ability to meet the rigorous requirements of your institution's renowned program in environmental science.

~~~~~ * ~~~~~ * ~~~~~ * ~~~~~ * ~~~~~

Ms. Li is widely respected throughout our company owing to her congenial personality and willingness to help when called upon.

~~~~~ * ~~~~~ * ~~~~~ * ~~~~~ * ~~~~~

Again, I am completely confident in Ms. Chiang's ability to satisfy your graduate programs' curriculum requirements. Please contact me if I can be of any further assistance.

~~~~~ * ~~~~~ * ~~~~~ * ~~~~~ * ~~~~~

I am quite confident that Ms. Ling can fully satisfy the rigorous requirements of your graduate school and, without hesitation, recommend her for admission to your school. Feel free to contact me if I can provide you with any further information about this highly motivated candidate

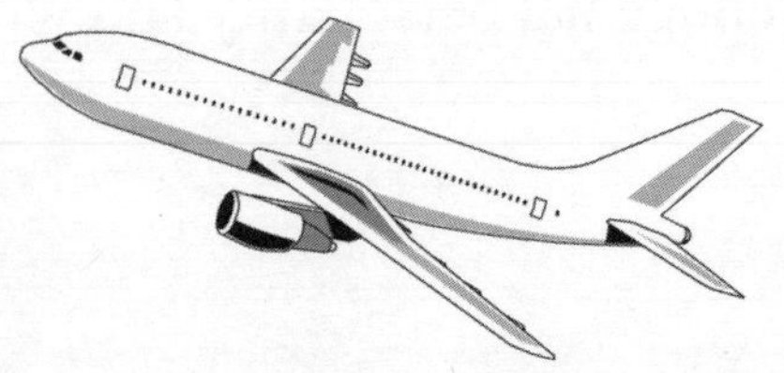
~~~~~

Answer Key

解 答

Unit One

Answer Key

Expressing interest in a field of study
表達學習領域興趣

A.

Situation 1

Wen is fascinated with the Internet's impact on all aspects of modern commerce. This fascination has resulted in near completion of a Master's degree in Computer Science with a concentration in network applications from National Tsing Hua University, one of Taiwan's premier institutes of higher learning. Upon completion of this degree, he will immediately pursue a Ph.D. in the same field, hopefully at UCLA.

Situation 2

Since childhood, May has dreamed of a world free of pollution and, as a result, has become an environmentally conscious individual. The strong research fundamentals acquired during her undergraduate years at National Cheng Chi University have prepared her for advanced study in Public Administration. Her graduate school research will hopefully center on how the government can implement environmentally friendly practices. Furthermore, she plans to identify those governmental measures that are vital to Taiwan's industrial sector. Moreover, she intends to actively participate in developing environmental protection laws for Taiwan.

Situation 3

Immersing himself in customer service-related issues, Ray has studied Marketing since high school. His particular interests are the increasing number of customer-oriented administrative database systems and customer/supplier relations. Thus, he wishes to further his knowledge through graduate studies on interactive marketing research, which is a timely topic for the recently emerging electronic communications media in Taiwan.

Situation 4

Sue has long been intrigued by creative, strategic decision making. Careful selection of which methods to adopt and actions to enforce in order to ensure that the best decision is made is what will make her a successful business manager. If admitted to the Management research program at MIT, she intends to concentrate on total systems intervention, including related issues of organizational processes, design, and culture. This explains why MIT was her first choice for doctoral studies. In addition to a distinguished Business Administration program, MIT's renowned research in contemporary management strategies such as business process re-engineering, quality management and total systems intervention is widely recognized. Sue's strong academic performance and solid background in Business Management have prepared her to meet the rigorous challenges of MIT's program.

B.

NOTE: The following are possible questions.

1. What are some contemporary management strategies that MIT is renowned for researching?
   Business process re-engineering, quality management and total systems intervention

2. What has Sue long been intrigued by?
   Creative, strategic decision making

3. What is Ray interested in studying?
   The increasing number of customer-oriented administrative database systems and customer/supplier relations.

C.

NOTE: The following are possible questions.

1. Which university provided May with strong research fundamentals?
   National Cheng Chi University

2. Which University does Wen hope to pursue a Ph.D. in Computer Science?
   UCLA

3. Which field has May prepared for advanced study in?
   Public Administration

D.

1. **What issues related to total systems intervention is Sue interested in studying?**

2. **From what university has Wen nearly completed a Master's degree in Computer Science?**

3. **What does May hope that her graduate school research will center on?**

F.

1. A major market for Taiwanese products in the near future will obviously be provided by China's population of over 1 billion people.

China's population of over 1 billion people will obviously provide a major market for Taiwanese products in the near future.

2. Heavy dependence on exports is a characteristic feature of Taiwan's economy.

Taiwan's economy heavily depends on exports.

3. Intervention in stock market fluctuations is often made by the Taiwanese government.

The Taiwanese government often intervenes in stock market fluctuations.

4. Strong analytical skills of applicants is a heavy emphasis of graduate school admission committees.

Graduate school admission committees heavily emphasize strong analytical skills of applicants.

5. Careful screening of all candidates is made by the admissions committee.

The admissions committee carefully screens all candidates.

6. Long term damage may be caused by these harmful practices.

The harmful practices may cause long term damage.

7. Development of sound fiscal policies by our nation's economists is necessary.

Our nation's economists must develop sound fiscal policies.

8. Keeping abreast of the latest changes in regulations and technological innovations is of essential concern to economists.

Economists must keep abreast of the latest changes in regulations and technological innovations.

9. Integrating knowledge in research and policy in the multi-disciplinary field of human development is rare in Graduate programs in Taiwan.

Graduate programs in Taiwan rarely integrate knowledge in research and policy in the multi-disciplinary field of human development.

10. The software may be difficult for users without a computer background to install.

Users without a computer background may have difficulty in installing the software.

Unit Two

Answer Key

Displaying current knowledge of a field of study

展現已有的學習領域知識（精確寫作：動詞代替名詞）

A.

Situation 1

With Taiwan's widely anticipated entry into the World Trade Organization its economy will undoubtedly witness unprecedented growth and greater access to global markets. Moreover, China's population of over 1 billion people may provide a major market for Taiwanese products in the near future, thus offering endless possibilities for market expansion. These exciting times in global economics explain why John has decided to study for a Ph.D. in Management as a logical extension to eventually commence a career in related research.

Situation 2

Taiwan heavily depends on international trade owing to its limited natural resources and domestic supply as well as demand in either the capital or commodity market. To fulfill its aspirations of becoming the financial center of the Asian Pacific region, Taiwan is facing deregulation and globalization. Taiwan is becoming more sensitive to fluctuating international markets, thus forging closer relations with other countries. Currently, Taiwan's most urgent need is for local economists to develop expert and comparative abilities, which match the rapid changes in regulation and innovation, such as those in the United States. Therefore, Susan has decided to pursue a graduate degree in International Finance.

Situation 3

Comparing urban and rural areas, Taiwan has an unequal distribution of urban public health resources. In particular, inadequate teaching faculties and libraries in these remote areas result in fewer high school graduates as well as an inferior standard of medical care. Inadequate health care available in these areas is further evidenced in the prevalence of severe health problems such as alcoholism and various infectious diseases. Equitable health care is essential for a productive and secure society. This explains why Tom has decided to devote himself to effectively addressing public health issues in Taiwan following an advanced degree at the Institute of Public Health at Harvard University.

Situation 4

Taiwan's economy has flourished in recent decades, as evidenced by rapid industrial expansion and market deregulation. Although the island escaped the Asian economic turmoil of the late 1990s relatively unscathed, a surging gross domestic product as well as an increasing emphasis on environmental issues has strained entrepreneurial development. Growing up in such an economically dynamic environment has motivated Nancy's interest in researching the way in which domestic companies can compete with multinational corporations and how the Taiwan government can adjust financial market strategies to enhance local competitiveness. Moreover, as Taiwan faces the reconstruction of its financial markets, identifying appropriate deregulations is essential. Therefore,

Nancy has decided to complete a Masters degree in International Finance.

B.

NOTE: The following are possible questions.

1. What are some major health problems in the rural areas of Taiwan?

   Alcoholism and various infectious diseases.

2. What degree has John decided to study for?

   A Ph.D. in Management

3. What factors have contributed to the flourishing of Taiwan's economy in recent decades?

   Rapid industrial expansion and market deregulation

C.

NOTE: The following are possible questions.

1. Which topic is Susan interested in?

   How to develop expert and comparative abilities, which match the rapid changes in regulation and innovation, such as those in the United States

2. Which country has underwent rapid changes in regulation and innovation?

   The United States

3. Which area is Taiwan becoming more sensitive to?

   Fluctuating international markets

D.

1. **Where has Tom decided to pursue an advanced degree?**

2. **What is Nancy interested in researching?**

3. **Is equitable health care essential for a productive and secure society?**

F.

1. Difficulty is faced in description of personal strengths to the admissions committee by applicants.

Applicants have difficulty in describing personal strengths to the admissions committee.

2. Recommendation of the applicant for graduate study is made by the department chairman.

The department chairman recommends the applicant for graduate study.

3. A significant increase in the number of applicants to graduate school has occurred in recent years.

The number of applicants to graduate school has significantly increased in recent years.

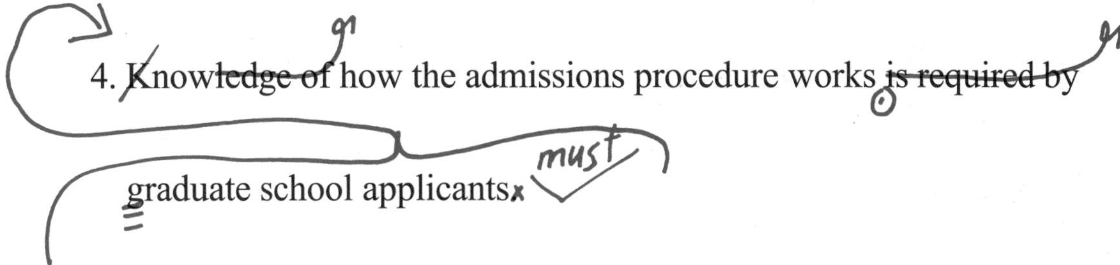
4. Knowledge of how the admissions procedure works is required by graduate school applicants.

Graduate school applicants must know how the admissions procedure works.

5. Not only is the academic record of an applicant considered by the admissions committee, but execution of related procedures is performed by that same committee.

In addition to considering the academic record of an applicant, the admissions committee must execute related procedures.

6. A recommendation of accepting Tom as a graduate student for pursuit of a doctorate degree in Finance was made by the committee chairman.

The committee chairman recommended accepting Tom as a graduate student to pursue a doctorate degree in Finance.

7. Selection of a career is achieved by an evaluation of available options.

A career is selected by evaluating available options.

8. An increase of career opportunities occurs by enhancement of one's computer skills.

Career opportunities increase by enhancing one's computer skills.

9. A stipulation by the admissions committee is that the forms be handed in by applicants no later than December 1st.

The admissions committee stipulates that applicants hand in the forms no later than December 1st.

10. Awareness of the changing economic climate is a must for job job applicants when looking for employment.

Job applicants must be aware of the changing economic climate when looking for employment.

Unit Three

Answer Key

Describing academic background and achievements

描述學歷背景及已獲成就

A.

Situation 1

After passing a highly competitive nationwide university entrance examination, Bill was admitted to the Commerce Department at National Cheng Kung University in 1999 where he majored in Finance. Several academic awards, an overall academic ranking of first out of a class of 300 and a cumulative GPA of 3.95/4.0 attest to his strong analytical skills and research fundamentals that he developed in order to conduct finance-related research. Upon graduation, he refused several employment offers in the financial sector to continue studies in commerce. This solid undergraduate training has equipped him for the rigorous demands of advanced study in this field.

Situation 2

A solid academic background in Industrial Engineering at one of Taiwan's premier universities, National Chiao Tung University, provided Ellen with the fundamental skills required for advanced research. Courses of particular interest during university were Manufacturing Process, Manufacturing Engineering, Production Planning and Control, as well as Industrial Organization and Management. Coursework during her junior and senior years in these areas heavily emphasized practical applications, often providing her with many opportunities to come into contact with actual enterprises.

Situation 3

John graduated from the Industrial Engineering Department at Feng Chia University in 1999. The departmental curricula provided him with a theoretical and practical understanding of industrial occupations, especially those in the electronics, telecommunications and semiconductor industries. Moreover, courses such as Quality Control and Factory Automation were particularly helpful in fostering his ability to solve problems logically.

In addition, John served as a research assistant in a National Science Council sponsored project on factory automation in Taiwan. Theoretical knowledge and practical laboratory experiences fostered his interest in this field of study even though limited resources and facilities prevented him from an in depth investigation. He also served as a teaching assistant for a course in quality management, which gave him a further glimpse into the dynamic nature of industry-related research.

Situation 4

During graduate school, Becky participated in several National Science Council research projects related to deregulation of the banking industry in Taiwan and its financial impact. Fully engaging in each stage of the projects, from original concept formation and experimental process design to experimental implementation, not only improved her research skills but also deepened her knowledge of related fields. She also attended many domestic and international conferences. These valuable experiences were very helpful when she wrote her master's thesis, a work having received considerable praise.

B.

NOTE: These are only possible answers.

1. Which major did Bill select at National Cheng Kung University?
   Finance

2. Which courses were Ellen interested in at National Chiao Tung University?
   Manufacturing Process, Manufacturing Engineering, Production Planning and Control as well as Industrial Organization and Management.

3. Which courses fostered John's ability to solve problems logically?
   Quality Control and Factory Automation

C.

NOTE: These are only possible answers.

1. What department did John graduate from in 1999?
   The Industrial Engineering Department at Feng Chia University.

2. What was Bill's overall academic ranking and cumulative GPA?
   First out of a class of 300 and a cumulative GPA of 3.95/4.0.

3. What did Becky attend during graduate school?
   Many domestic and international conferences

D.

1. Why does Bill want to develop his analytical skills and research fundamentals?

2. Did the departmental curricula in the Industrial Engineering Department at Feng Chia University provide John with a theoretical and practical understanding of industrial occupations, especially those in the electronics, telecommunications and semiconductor industries?

3. Why did Bill refuse several employment opportunities in the fiancial sector?

F.

1. No significant difference in test scores occurred between the two groups.

The two groups did not significantly differ in test scores.

2. The gross domestic product was not significantly different between the two countries.

The two countries did not significantly differ in gross domestic product.

3. The performance is only a little affected by adjustment of the temperature.

Adjusting the temperature only slightly affects the performance.

4. An increase in government funding causes the student drop out rate to decrease.

Increasing government funding decreases the student drop out rate.

5. The larger the university, the more diverse its student population.

The larger the university implies a more diverse student population.

6. The instructor placed an emphasis on how modern management practices are related.

The instructor emphasized how modern management practices are related.

7. First year graduate students must make an adjustment of their research interests according to their advisor's suggestions.

First year graduate students must adjust their research interests according to their advisor's suggestions.

8. The committee members give a recommendation whether or not to accept the applicants.

The committee members recommend whether or not to accept the applicants.

9. Completion of the admissions process is required by all committee members so that objectivity can be ensured.

All committee members must complete the admissions process to ensure objectivity.

10. Acceptance to a particular graduate school program is heavily dependent on the candidate's academic performance.

Acceptance to a particular graduate school program heavily depends on the candidate's academic performance.

Answer Key

Introducing research and professional experiences
介紹研究及工作經驗

A.

Situation 1

As an undergraduate student, John participated in technology management-related research, with a particular emphasis on how modern management practices are related. Those findings culminated in publication of a research paper. To enhance his research abilities, he attended several international conferences and audited management courses at the Institute of Technology Management at National Taiwan University.

Situation 2

Julie's studies at the Institute of Food Research at National Taiwan Normal University provided her not only with solid background knowledge of diet and nutrition, but also with the desire to become an academic researcher in this exciting field. While working on her bachelor's degree, she joined the Food Safety Laboratory to understand how food poisoning affects humans. This experience reinforced her dedication to laboratory work and highlighted the importance of developing pertinent research questions and experimental designs that enable data analysis.

Situation 3

Larry's current research project involves designing a questionnaire, interviewing study participants and analyzing data. These experiences offer a glimpse into the dynamic nature of educational research and the exciting challenges of a research career. Although his aspiration of becoming a distinguished researcher will be an arduous journey, he is ready to immerse himself in academia. Moreover, Larry believes that he has the intellect and determination to meet its challenges.

Situation 4

As a physical therapist at Chang Gung Memorial Hospital for the past five years, Cathy finds her work with physically challenged individuals as personally fulfilling since she can facilitate their improvement through therapy. In addition to providing therapy for children, Cathy has gained advanced professional knowledge and, thus, believes that graduate study would further improve upon it. Moreover, she believes that a medical professional who is undertaking research to examine therapeutic changes requires the skills to design and conduct a study.

B.

NOTE: These are only possible answers.

1. Where did Julie work at while working on her bachelor's degree?
   The Food Safety Laboratory

2. Where does Cathy work as a physical therapist?
   Chang Gung Memorial Hospital

3. Where did John go to enhance his research abilities?
   Several international conferences

C.

NOTE: These are only possible answers.

1. What does Cathy believe a clinical practitioner who is undertaking research needs to examine therapeutic changes?
   The skills to design and conduct a study

2. What was the emphasis of John's technology management-related research as an undergraduate student?
   How modern management practices are related

3. What does Larry's current research project involve?
   Designing a questionairre, interviewing student participants and analyzing data.

D.

1. What does Larry believe he has to meet the challenges of becoming a distinguished researcher?

2. Why does Cathy find her work with physically challenged individuals as personally fulfilling?

3. Why did Julie join the Food Safety Laboratory?

F.

1. It is likely that the price of a private school education is higher than that of a public one.

A private school education likely costs more than a public one.

2. There is a need for control of the number of graduate students admitted each fall semester by the faculty committee.

The faculty committee must control the number of graduate students admitted each fall semester.

3. It is essential that cooperation with each other is the goal of research team members.

Research team members must aim to cooperate with each other.

OR simply say

Research team members must cooperate with each other.

4. It may happen that a decision to not attend a particular graduate school program is made by the applicant.

The applicant may decide not to attend a particular graduate school.

5. There is a necessity for an agreement on the research topic by the graduate school advisor and advisee.

The graduate school advisor and advisee must agree on the research topic.

6. It is critical that consideration of all available research programs is made by the graduate school applicant.

The graduate school applicant must consider all available research programs.

7. It is crucial that careful assessment of the candidate's academic potential is made by the admissions committee.

The admissions committee must carefully assess the candidate's academic potential.

8. It is not necessary for the presentation of a detailed research proposal be made by students in their graduate school application.

Students do not need to present a detailed research proposal in their graduate school application.

9. There is increasing evidence that suggests there is a relation between academic performance and nutrition.

Increasing evidence suggests that academic performance and nutrition are related.

10. ~~There is a~~ limitation ~~on~~ the number of words in a Statement of Purpose for graduate study ~~by~~ many admissions committees.

Many admissions committees limit the number of words in a Statement of Purpose for graduate study.

Unit Five

Answer Key

Describing extracurricular activities relevant to study
描述與學習有關的課外活動

A.

Situation 1

During university, Jerry participated in a social service organization that held summer youth camps. After several years of participation, he gradually assumed a leading role in planning the program of these youth camps. While providing sports, entertainment, and art-related activities, these camps equip students with communicative skills, provide exposure to peers on an equal footing and broaden their horizons.

Executing such a comprehensive camp schedule requires close collaboration among team members to ensure success. As a leader, Jerry had to initiate innovative ways of keeping volunteers involved, such as planning special dinners to coincide with planning sessions, using a sense of humor to retain everyone's interest, making related tasks enjoyable and, above all, providing an example of hard work for others to follow. This unique leadership opportunity was one of the most rewarding experiences of his undergraduate years.

Situation 2

The many extracurricular activities that Betty participated in during university gave her the necessary balance of developing academic and social skills simultaneously. She often served as a representative or spokesperson of campus organizations, subsequently making many new friends and building her self-confidence. In addition to a solid academic background, a good manager should have strong communicative, organizational and management skills. Also, the fact that she is bilingual allowed her to easily adjust to different cultures and understand how different market niches fit in the larger global picture.

Situation 3

Realizing that the medical profession should actively educate communities and society to avoid the spread of social diseases, Tom worked with other classmates in organizing an AIDS awareness campaign on the university campus to make students more aware of the devastating effects of this disease and preventive measures. Implementing this project brought him into contact with various entities such as school administrators and shop owners, thus sharpening his negotiation skills and showing him the discrepancy between theory and practice. This diverse education strengthened and broadened his solid knowledge base, and further enhanced his sensitivity towards various medical issues.

Situation 4

Serving as the public relations chairperson of a fundraising campaign for global hunger was a turning point in Sally's decision to pursue a career in marketing. This challenging work broadened her horizons by allowing her to coordinate a large scale marketing and promotion project for a good cause. While increasing her interest in the field of communications, this experience also made her confident of her ability to achieve career goals by applying knowledge skills in a systematic manner. Taiwan lacks individuals with both hands on experience and sufficient knowledge skills to market products in an integrated and efficient manner. This need has inspired Sally to pursue an advanced degree in Marketing Management in the United States.

B.

NOTE: These are only possible answers.

1. Where did Tom work with other classmates in organizing an AIDS awareness program?
   On the university campus

2. Where is there a lack of individuals with both hands on experience and sufficient knowledge skills to market products in an integrated and efficient manner?
   Taiwan

3. Where did Betty learn the necessary balance of developing academic and social skills simultaneously?
   The many extracurricular activities that she participated in during university.

C.

NOTE: These are only possible answers.

1. What does Betty believe a good manager should have?
   A solid academic background as well as strong communicative, organizational and management skills

2. What was the turning point in Sally's decision to pursue a career in marketing?
   When she served as the public relations chairperson of a fundraising campaign for global hunger.

3. What was one of Jerry's most rewarding experiences of his undergraduate years?
   Participating in a social organization that held summer youth camps.

D.

1. What allows Betty to easily adjust to different cultures and how different market niches fit in the larger global picture?

2. How did Betty make many new friends and build her self-confidence?

3. How did Tom try to make students aware of the devastating effects of AIDS and preventive measures?

F.

Match the unclear word or phrase with the concise one. The first one has been done for you.

Unclear	Concise
In many cases	never
in most cases	if
in no case	consider, examine
for this reason	exceeds
give consideration to	several, many
give indication of	if
happens to be	am/is/are
if conditions are such that	indicate/suggest
in a number of	to, for
in close proximity to	because, since
is in excess of	always
in large measure	so
in all cases	near
in case	thus, therefore
accordingly	largely
for the purpose of	often
for the reason that	usually

Match the unclear word or phrase with the concise one.
The first one has been done for you.

Unclear	Concise
reach a conclusion	after
serves the function of	how
subsequent to	ask about, inquire about
it is interesting that	conclude
it is our opinion that	although
manner in which	notably
notwithstanding the fact that	we believe
on the basis of	may, might, could, can
put an end to	is
the question as to	if
on the order of	about, approximately
prior to	from, because, by
provided that	whether
it is possible that	before
make inquiry regarding	interestingly
it is noted that	end

Match the unclear word or phrase with the concise one. The first one has been done for you.

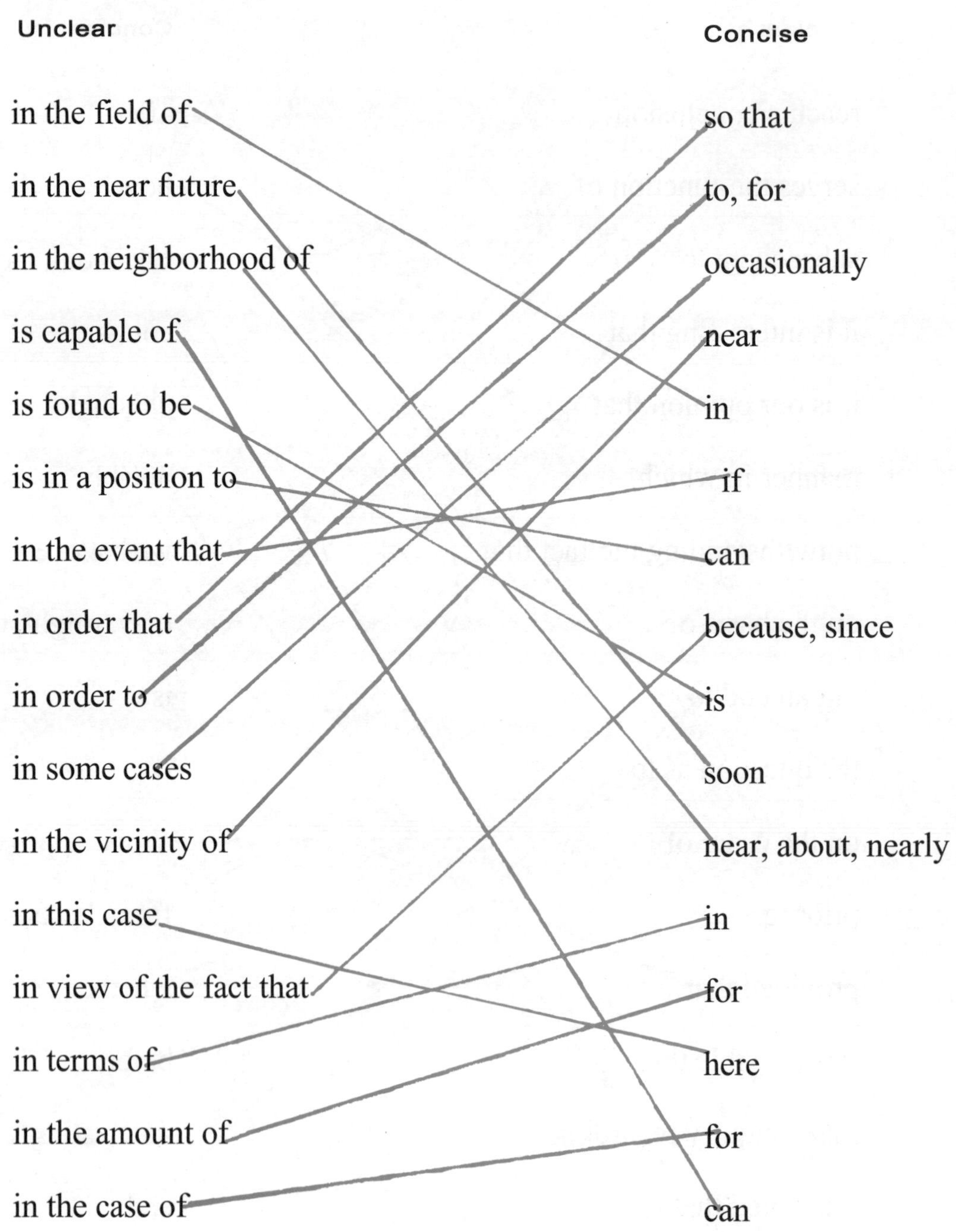

Match the unclear word or phrase with the concise one.
The first one has been done for you.

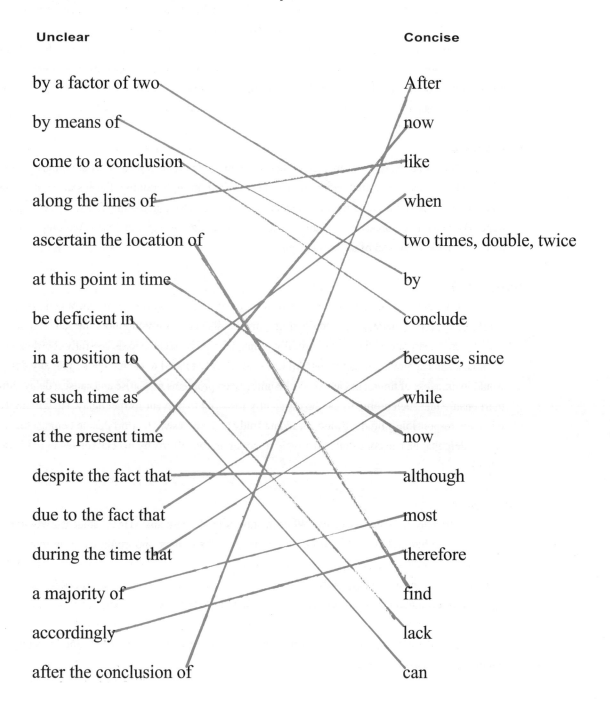

Unclear	Concise
by a factor of two	After
by means of	now
come to a conclusion	like
along the lines of	when
ascertain the location of	two times, double, twice
at this point in time	by
be deficient in	conclude
in a position to	because, since
at such time as	while
at the present time	now
despite the fact that	although
due to the fact that	most
during the time that	therefore
a majority of	find
accordingly	lack
after the conclusion of	can

Unit Six

Answer Key

Describing personal qualities relevant to study
描述與學習有關的個人特質

A.

Situation 1

Patrick's academic performance during university is a notable example of his diligence. Despite his undistinguished academic work during the first two years of university, he was determined to raise his grade point average beginning with the first semester of his senior year. However, he did not flinch from taking rigorous courses such as Finance, Accounting and Economics. Moreover, he received final course grades of 80 or higher during his last two years of university. In addition to coursework, his personal actions reflect his desire to be a high achiever.

Situation 2

Ann's superiors have often commented on her ingenuity in approaching complex situations. While some feel that this is inherited, creativity can be nurtured through training. For instance, she is in tune with popular trends and often distinguishes between a passing marketing fad and an emerging trend. By remaining abreast of consumer behavior for a target group, Ann can often pinpoint the untapped market demand of a certain group.

Situation 3

Jim's colleagues and superiors can attest to his responsible and trustworthy character. When assigned a task, he quickly generates a schedule, drafts the details and closely monitors the schedule until completion. He strongly believes that carefully planned timing is essential to successfully coordinating work tasks and achieving target goals. All tasks are closely related to each other so that any delay would incur a loss of timing or capital. While unforeseen problems may arise and cause a delay, Jim must ensure that such problems can be efficiently resolved to prevent further delay. He will apply this same responsible attitude towards graduate study and any research effort that he belongs to. He is confident that he can contribute positively to collaborative efforts by his classmates in graduate school.

Situation 4

Tammy is friendly and communicative. While in university, she participated in the student government association in her department. During that period, she had many opportunities to interact with individuals from diverse backgrounds and could easily accommodate herself within a group. In both of her jobs, she had to frequently communicate with superiors, clients, agents, speakers, scholars and experts. Communication skills were nurtured, allowing her to assess different situations rationally. Graduate school will provide Tammy with many opportunities to collaborate and interact with classmates and professors, as well as even occasionally meet with entrepreneurs. She feels highly competent in such situations.

B.

NOTE: These are only possible answers.

1. What did Tammy have many opportunities to do in university?
   To interact with individuals from diverse backgrounds

2. What opportunities will graduate school provide Tammy?
   To collaborate and interact with classmates and professors, even occasionally meeting with entrepreneurs.

3. What were some of the rigorous courses that Patrick took in university?
   Finance, Accounting and Economics

C.

NOTE: These are only possible answers.

1. Can Jim's colleagues and superiors attest to his responsible and trustworthy character?
   Yes

2. Was Patrick an outstanding student during his first two years of university?
   No.

3. Did Tammy participate in extracurricular activities in university?
   Yes

D.

1. What does Ann often distinguish between?

2. What does Ann believe can be nurtured through training?

3. Who did Tammy have to frequently communicate with in both of her jobs?

F.

1. A number of graduate schools (has, have) offered writing courses for first year graduate students who are non-native English speakers.

2. A graduate school applicant that (chooses, choose) to provide ample information that is relevant to his or her academic background (allows, allow) the admissions committee to more easily evaluate the potential of that individual to fulfill course requirements.

3. Determination along with intelligence significantly (affects, affect) a graduate student's academic performance.

4. Neither extracurricular activities nor academic background solely (determines, determine) acceptance to graduate school.

5. To express interest in a field of study and display current knowledge of that field (is, are) essential for an effective study plan.

6. Telecommunications (is , are) a newly emerging field in Taiwan's industrial sector.

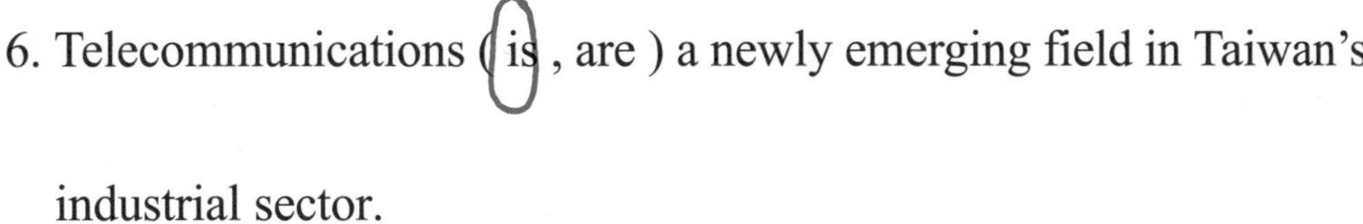

7. Each of the points in this book (contributes , contribute) to a successful study plan.

8. The procedure in which students (follows , follow) to gain Admittance to graduate school (requires , require) much patience.

9. Outlining one's career objectives in addition to stating why a particular institution is selected for advanced study (plays , play) an important part in describing one's study plan.

10. The number of admissions committees that require a study plan (has, have) increased in recent years.

Unit Seven

Answer Key

Outlining career objectives
概述未來工作目標

A.

Situation 1

After completing the masters degree program in Strategic Management from the University of Florida, Richard will return to Taiwan to make a more significant contribution than he would be able to do without further academic training. He plans to work in a multinational corporation or research institute. Marketing strategy, research methodology and logical thinking - all of these skills nurtured in the masters program - will enable him to effectively respond to the latest technological advances in the workplace. His exposure to case studies as well as statistical and theoretical analysis in the masters program will make him more receptive to novel concepts. Such diverse work experiences, combined with a masters degree, will hopefully place him in line for a managerial position in just a few years.

Situation 2

Following successful completion of MITs academic requirements, Jill plans to work for roughly three to five years as a marketing strategist, preferably analyzing potential markets to enhance export growth. This work will hopefully enable her to more thoroughly understand emerging markets in Taiwan and to establish an extensive personal network to facilitate ongoing research. Beyond that initial five years, she hopes to contribute to her country through researching new marketing theories and, perhaps, through helping the government construct sounder strategic policies. Jill also plans to teach marketing theory so that more people can contribute to Taiwan's competitiveness in global markets.

Situation 3

After successfully completing a master's degree from UCLA, Bill plans to continue with his studies until he has eventually earned a doctorate degree in social work. Doing so would allow him to be in a better position to promote the quality of social work in Taiwan. He is especially interested in child care and family law.

Situation 4

Upon completion of her graduate degree, Mary hopes to return to Taiwan and seek a teaching position in a junior college or university. By acquiring advanced knowledge and specialized skills that New York University offers, she will be better equipped and confident to take on such a position. As well, her experiences gained through the graduate program at New York University will also benefit the development of information systems in Taiwan, which has recently began to focus on improving and revising software processes.

B.

NOTE: These are only possible questions.

1. Why is Richard interested in marketing strategy, research methodology and logical thinking?
   To effectively respond to the latest technological advances in the workplace.

2. Why is Mary interested in acquiring advanced knowledge and specialized skills?
   To be better equipped and confident to take on a teaching position in a junior college or university.

3. Why does Jill plan to work about three to five years as a marketing strategist?
   To more thoroughly understand emerging markets in Taiwan and to establish an extensive personal network to facilitate ongoing research.

C.

NOTE: These are only possible questions.

1. What does Mary hope to do after she completes her graduate degree?
   Return to Taiwan

2. What would Jill like to do in contributing to her country?
   Researching new marketing theories and helping the government construct sounder strategic policies.

3. What career is Bill interested in?
   Social work

D.

1. Where does Mary hope to pursue an advanced degree?

2. What has the development of information systems in Taiwan recently began to focus on?

3. What will Richard be exposed to in the masters program that will make him more receptive to novel concepts?

F.

1. It is the responsibility of the committee chairman to supervise all admissions procedures.

The committee chairman is responsible for supervising all admissions procedures.

2. It is well known that preparing a rough draft of the study plan allows applicants to present their ideas more thoroughly.

As well known, preparing a rough draft of the study plan allows applicants to present their ideas more thoroughly.

3. The admissions process takes a considerable amount of time, which implies that all submitted materials are carefully reviewed.

The admissions process takes a considerable amount of time, implying that all submitted materials are carefully reviewed.

4. In a study plan, it is expected that applicants to describe the motivation for pursuing an advanced degree.

When writing a study plan, applicants are expected to describe the motivation for pursuing an advanced degree.

5. In Taiwan's telecommunications industry, they are applying advanced technologies because the island has a globally competitive export market.

Taiwan's telecommunications industry is applying advanced technologies because the island has a globally competitive export market.

6. They stated in their report how admissions procedures should be changed.

Their report stated how admissions procedures should be changed.

7. When admissions committees apply different standards for selecting candidates, they have difficulty in achieving a uniform criteria.

When applying different standards for selecting candidates, admissions committees have difficulty in achieving a uniform criteria

8. They demonstrated in an earlier investigation that graduate school applicants tend to reveal personal qualities that reflect academic potential for advanced study.

An earlier investigation demonstrated that graduate school applicants tend to reveal personal qualities that reflect academic potential for advanced study.

9. It is widely recognized that the accounting program at Indiana University consistently ranks high in national surveys.

As widely recognized, the accounting program at Indiana University consistently ranks high in national surveys.

10. It is the assumption of the admissions committee that all submitted materials are original.

The admissions committee assumes that all submitted materials are original.

Answer Key

Stating why an institution was selected for advanced study
解釋選擇該校原由

A.

Situation 1

To achieve his career aspirations, Richard intends to enhance his education through a graduate degree program at an American university. From conversations with classmates, as well as numerous professors and industry figures, he has concluded that graduate study in the United States would be the most effective means to achieve the training that he will need as a leader in the organization that he is currently working in. Admissions to the MA degree program in Internet Marketing at the University of Oregon will foster the skills Richard needs to fully realize his aspiration of becoming an information specialist in the marketing field. Graduate study is the logical next step to fully realizing his career potential. The solid graduate curricula program at the University of Oregon will build upon and refine the fundamental skills that he gained during undergraduate study.

Situation 2

Mary began searching for a graduate school in which she can achieve her career goals. Via the Internet, periodicals and magazines in her university library, she discovered that the accounting program at Indiana University, a graduate program that has consistently ranked high in national surveys, is the one she was looking for. What attracted her the most was the highly qualified and experienced faculty with frequent publications in prestigious journals, seemingly unlimited academic resources, as well as its distinctive and unique tradition. Mary believes that logical thinking is essential to professionalism in accounting and Indiana University's program in this area would provide her with the knowledge required to achieve her ambitions. In addition, the weather and geographical conditions are pleasing to her.

Situation 3

To achieve the above aspirations, applying to the prestigious Department of Chemical Engineering is the logical choice for Larry. The diverse and professional curricula is what attracts him the most to the University of Washington. He is particularly drawn to the university's programs that focus on equipping its graduates with the technical competence and flexibility necessary to effectively respond to challenges within the chemical engineering profession. Larry feels that he has the talent, insight, intelligence, creativity, and potential to contribute to the rich pool of talented individuals at the University of Washington. With a solid background in Chemistry along with his strong interests in the field, he is also confident that he can significantly contribute to any research team that he belongs to.

Situation 4

Graduate study in the United States would equip Melody with the necessary skills to thrive in the workplace. Taiwan's economy has flourished since 1970, as evidenced by rapid industrial expansion and market deregulation. While the island passed through the Asian economic turmoil of the late

1990s relatively unscathed, its revenues generated from information products and its average stock trading volume rank third and fifth worldwide, respectively. Growing up in such an economically vibrant environment has motivated Melody's interest to more fully understand how domestic companies compete with multinational corporations and how Taiwan's government can adjust financial markets to enhance local competitiveness. Her review of numerous journal articles has led her to understand the dominant role that the United States plays in developing related theories and applications.

B.

NOTE: These are only possible answers.

1. Where did economic turmoil occur in the late 1990's?
   Asia

2. Where is Richard heading to fully realize his aspiration of becoming an information specialist?
   Graduate school

3. Where would Mary like to pursue a graduate degree in Accounting?
   Indiana University

C.

NOTE: These are only possible answers.

1. What graduate program has consistently ranked high in national surveys?
   The accounting program at Indiana University

2. What university department is Larry drawn to?
   The Department of Chemical Engineering at the University of Washington.

3. What does Richard aspire to become?
   An information specialist in the marketing field

D.

1. **What is the logical next step for Richard to fully realize his career potential?**
   Graduate study

2. **What pleases Mary about the location of Indiana University?**
   Its weather and geographical conditions.

3. **What does Larry have?**
   A solid background in Chemistry

F.

1. The study plan is promising, creative, and the author writes well.

The study plan is promising, creative, and well written.

2. The committee made a decision to accept six candidates and that the meeting should be adjourned.

The committee decided to accept six candidates and to adjourn the meeting.

3. Graduate students select a research topic under the guidance of their advisors and deadlines are set to monitor progress of the thesis project.

Graduate students select a research topic under the guidance of their advisors and set deadlines to monitor progress of the thesis project.

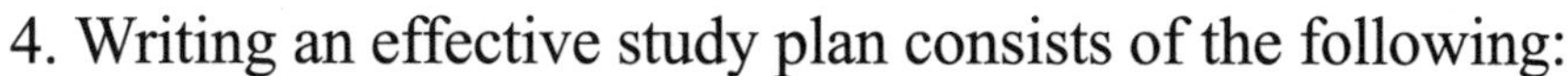

4. Writing an effective study plan consists of the following:

Expressing interest in a field of study,

Displaying current knowledge of that field,

Academic bacground and achievements are described,

Research and professional experiences are introduced,

Describing extracurricular activities relevant to study, and

Personal qualities relevant to study are described,

Writing an effective study plan consists of the following:
Expressing interest in a field of study,
Displaying current knowledge of that field,
Describing academic background and achievements,
Introducing research and professional experiences,
Describing extracurricular activities relevant to study, and
Describing personal qualities relevant to study.

5. Most study plans neither require a detailed outline for the thesis project nor must a literature review be provided.

Most study plans neither require a detailed outline for the thesis project nor provide a literature review.

6. The study plan should outline career objectives and explaining the reason for selecting that institution.

The study plan should outline career objectives and explain the reason for selecting that institution.

7. The study plan should also describe extracurricular activities that are relevant to study and that research and professional experiences are introduced as well.

The study plan should also describe extracurricular activities that are relevant to study and introduce research and professional experiences as well.

8. The previous approach is complicated, inefficient and wastes too much time.

The previous approach is complicated, inefficient and time consuming.

9. Effective study plans make a description of an applicant's academic background and achievements as well as expressing interest in a field of study.

Effective study plans describe an applicant's academic background and achievements as well as express in a field of study.

10. The applicant focused on an introduction of her research and professional experiences and to display current knowledge of her field of interest.

The applicant focused on introducing her research and professional experiences and displaying current knowledge of her field of interest.

Answer Key

Recommending a student for study (Part A): Introduction and qualification to make recommendation

撰寫推薦信函(A部份)推薦信函開始及推薦人的資格

A.

Situation 1

As chairman of the Finance Department at National Tsing Hua University, Professor Chang had the opportunity to closely observe Mr. Johnny Li when he enrolled in his course in Global Economics. In addition to his exemplary academic performance, Mr. Li also served as the social chairman of the department's student association.

Situation 2

As chairman of the Technical Management program at Soochow University and a frequent reader of management reports, Professor Su must often point out errors in the report contents of undergraduate work and their overall quality. At the beginning of the semester, she often criticized the work of the team that Mr. Jerry Chang belonged to in her offered course of Total Quality Management. However, his team gradually progressed in its preparation and overall quality of work. In doing so, they provided valuable insight into the way in which total quality management is increasingly adopted in Taiwan's semiconductor industry, as documented in a report they wrote to fulfill the course requirements. Mr. Chang played an instrumental role in this team, not only in orally presenting group findings but also in assigning work to team members.

Situation 3

Professor Yu hopes that this recommendation letter aptly conveys his confidence in Miss Mary Li's ability to not only meet the academic requirements but excel in UCLA's master's degree program in Strategic Management. In addition to observing her academic performance while enrolled in his Advanced Accounting course during her junior year of university, Professor Yu also monitored her work performance in his accounting lab over the past six months.

Situation 4

Enrolled in Professor Wei's courses of Introduction to Art and Art Theory, Sherry Lu enthusiastically contributed to the class, subsequently inspiring other students to participate more actively. In addition, her excellent academic performance exceeded the professor's expectations from many years of teaching.

B.

NOTE: These are only possible questions.

1. Did Jerry Chang actively participate in Professor Su's offered course of Total Quality Management?
   Yes, he did.

2. Did Sherry Lu enthusiastically contribute to Professor Wei's courses of Engineering Management?
   No. She enthusiastically contributed to Professor Wei's courses of Introduction to Art and Art Theory.

3. Does Professor Yu have confidence in Mary Li's ability to excel in UCLA's master's degree program in Strategic Management?
   Yes.

C.

NOTE: These are only possible answers.

1. What is increasingly adopted in Taiwan's semiconductor industy?
   Total quality management
2. What must Professor Su often do as a frequent reader of management reports?
   He must often point out errors in the report contents of undergraduate work and their overall quality.
3. What kind of lab did Mary Li work in for the past six months?
   Accounting

D.

1. Did Jerry Chang orally present group findings in Professor Su's offered course of Total Quality Management?
   Yes.
2. When did Mary enroll in Professor Yu's course in Advanced Accounting?
   During her junior year
3. What effect did Sherry have on her classmates in Professor Wei's courses of Introduction to Art and Art Theory?
   She inspired students to participate more actively.

F.

1. To express interest in a field of study, a related background is strongly advised for an applicant.

   An applicant is strongly advised to have a related background when expressing interest in a field of study.

a student,

2. Before submitting a study plan, the institution should be selected.

Before a student submits a study plan, the institution should be selected.

3. When writing the study plan, personal qualities that reflect academic potential should be highlighted.

an applicant

When writing the study plan, an applicant should highlight personal qualities that reflect academic potential.

4. When describing extracurricular activities, their relevance to graduate study must be pointed out.

applicants

When describing extracurricular activities, applicants must point out their relevance to graduate study.

5. The study plan written by the applicant which was well structured was warmly received.

The well structured study plan written by the applicant was warmly received.

6. When stating why an institution is selected for advanced study, its reputation in a particular field should be mentioned.

When stating why an institution is selected for advanced study, applicants should mention its reputation in a particular field.

7. Before recommending a student for a graduate program, personal details of the applicant should be obtained.

Before recommending a student for a graduate program, the professor should obtain personal details of the applicant.

8. To outline one's career objectives in a study plan, a long term goal should be highlighted.

To outline one's career objectives in a study plan, an applicant should highlight a long term goal.

9. Having a large database, the latest information on graduate programs in France ~~can be found in~~ the campus network. contains

Having a large database, the campus network contains the latest information on graduate programs in France.

Unit Ten

Answer Key

Recommending a student for study (Part B): Personal qualities of the candidate that are relevant to

撰寫推薦信函（ B部份 ）被推薦人與進階學習有關的個人特質及信函結尾

A.

Situation 1

John Wang often served as a team leader in Professor Li's research group, frequently engaging other team members in discussion and assigning tasks. Professor Li largely attributes the team's excellent performance to John's persistent direction. Importantly, he appears to have learned the merit of carefully listening to others opinions, even when his views were in contrast to theirs.

Professor Li can not emphasize enough her confidence in Mr. Wang's ability and determination to successfully complete his graduate studies. In addition to his academic potential, a strong personality and effective communication skills will prove invaluable for the challenges of graduate study. The admissions committee should not hesitate to contact Professor Li if she can provide further insight into this highly qualified candidate.

Situation 2

Susan's diligent attitude towards studying never ceased to amaze Professor Lin. For instance, whenever encountering a bottleneck in her research progress, Susan always delved into reading and investigating the source of the problem while consulting with Professor Lin on how to resolve the problem at hand. On her own initiative, Susan continues to maintain contact with several researchers in the field, discussing relevant issues related to their clinical or research experiences. In addition, her critical thinking skills are remarkable, as evidenced by her ability to synthesize pertinent reading materials, identify the limitations of previous literature and then state the logical next step in research from a unique perspective. Moreover, her analytical skills are exemplary. Although unfamiliar with the research topic at the outset, she analyzed the most pertinent information within her field of interest and then identified the research questions and hypothesis.

Her creativity and cooperative nature will be a great asset to any future research effort that she belongs to. The opportunity to pursue advanced study in MIT's graduate program will allow her to undertake innovative research in chemical engineering. Professor Lin therefore has no hesitations in highly recommending this candidate for admissions into MIT's graduate program.

Situation 3

Betty constantly read upon related theory and discussed her observations with classmates. During weekly group meetings that involved journal discussions and case reports, she actively participated through her carefully thought out questions and responses to other participants' views.

In addition to her strong academic performance, Professor Smith was also impressed with her optimism. For instance, not only did she seek Professor Smith on finance-related matters, but she also sought out experts in the field to learn of their experiences. Such enthusiasm displays her determination to purse a career in Finance. Professor Smith holds no reservations in recommending this highly qualified candidate for admissions to the University of Michigan's graduate school.

Situation 4

Tom has been a research assistant at the research and development department for five years. He is responsible for performing various experimental procedures and analyzing those results. His diligence in collecting and organizing materials in the department has played an important role in the company's efforts to develop new computers. He has the unique ability to identify exactly what he lacks for a particular research objective. He also quickly understands the limitations of conventional research in a particular area. Moreover, he has enthusiastically undertook experiments, attempting to solve problems from different angles. Remaining confident despite occasional setbacks, Mr. Su remained persistent during experimental work, ultimately resulting in the establishment of a new process.

Furthermore, Tom has the keen ability to effectively address problems, as evidenced by his exemplary presentation skills and organizational skills during weekly meetings. His presentations were professionally delivered and well prepared.

With his vast laboratory experience, insight, and positive attitude towards eliminating ambiguity in mental health programs, I am highly confident of Tom's ability to satisfy the rigorous requirements of Harvard University's renowned program in computer science.

B.

NOTE: These are only possible questions.

1. What graduate school is Professor Smith recommending Betty to?
   The University of Michigan

2. What does Tom quickly understand?
   The limitations of conventional research in a particular area.

3. What graduate program is Susan applying to at MIT?
   Chemical Engineering.

C.

NOTE: These are only possible answers.

1. Why is Professor Change impressed with Susan's critical thinking skills?
   Owing to her ability to synthesize pertinent reading materials, identify the limitations of previous literature and then state the logical next step in research from a unique perspective.

2. Why is Tom qualified to meet the rigorous requirements of Harvard University's renowned program in Computer Science?

His vast laboratory experience, insight and positive attitude towards eliminating ambiguity in computer programs.

3. Why is Professor Smith recommeding Betty for graduate study?

Her strong academic performance and enthusiasm.

D.

1. What does Professor Li believe will prove invaluable for graduate study?

2. What did Susan always delve into when encountering a bottleneck in her research?

3. How long has Tom been a laboratory technician in the research and development department?

F.

1. Her study plan is more thorough with respect to knowledge of the field of study than those of other applicants.

Her study plan is more thorough with respect to knowledge of the field of study than those of other applicants.

2. The Chemistry Department comes into contact with school administration more than other departments do.

The Chemistry Department comes into contact with school administration more than other departments do.

as

3. The candidate's professional experiences are as in depth, if not more in depth than, other applicants.

The candidate's professional experiences are as in depth as, if notmore in depth than, those of other applicants.

4. The Chemistry Department's publications in international journals are

those of

more than the French Department.

The Chemistry department's publications in international journals are more than those of the French Department.

with

5. Sue has always been fascinated the way in which successful managers can think creatively when making decisions.

Sue has always been fascinated with the way in which successful managers can think creatively when making decisions.

6. Our proposal has a higher likelihood of success.

Our proposal has a higher likelihood of success than theirs.

7. The graduate school emphasizes journal publications more than the undergraduate one.

The graduate school emphasizes journal publications more than the undergraduate one does.

8. The acceptance rate at Jones University is as high, if not higher than, other public institutions.

The acceptance rate at Jones University is as high as, if not higher than, that at other public instituutions.

in

9. Jerry is interested studying organizational design.

Jerry is interested in studying organizational design.

that of

10. Thompson University's dropout rate is lower than St. Mary's University.

Thompson University's dropout rate is lower than that of St. Mary's University.

An Editing Checklist for Conciseness and Clarity

A. Conciseness

★ Use active voice frequently

A simple way to delete the length of a sentence and make it direct at the same time is to frequently use the active voice. Switching from passive voice to active voice often makes a sentence more direct, concise and persuasive. Whereas sentences using passive voice tend to be wordy or indecisive, sentences utilizing active voice make the technical document more immediate and concise. Consider the following examples:

就像先前所說，如何用最少的字來表達一個完整的意念通常是科技寫作者一個大挑戰，然而這裡有一個祕訣，那就是使用主動語法。請記住主動語氣使句子更直接，明確及更有說服力。

Original

Heavy dependence on exports is a characteristic feature of Taiwan's economy.

Revised

Taiwan's economy heavily depends on exports.

Original

Intervention in stock market fluctuations is often made by the Taiwanese government.

Revised

The Taiwanese government often intervenes in stock market fluctuations.

Original

Strong analytical skills of applicants is a heavy emphasis of graduate school admission committees.

Revised

Graduate school admission committees heavily emphasize strong analytical skills of applicants.

Original

Careful screening of all candidates is made by the admissions committee.

Revised

The admissions committee carefully screens all candidates.

★ **Use verbs instead of nouns**

Wordiness also comes from creating nouns out of verbs (known as nominalizations). This tendency leads to weak verbs. In addition, overuse of nouns instead of verbs also creates needless prepositions. Consider the following examples:

句子冗贅的原因也可能是使用太多的名詞，通常這些名詞是由動詞轉化來的，而結果是使動詞更無力，此部份會在第四單元詳論。此外，過份的濫用名詞也帶來了多餘的介係詞。細想以下例句：

Original
Knowledge of how the admissions procedure works is required by graduate school applicants.
Revised
Graduate school applicants must know how the admissions procedure works.

Original
Not only is the academic record of an applicant considered by the admissions committee, but execution of related procedures is performed by that same committee.
Revised
In addition to considering the academic record of an applicant, the admissions committee must execute related procedures.

Original
An increase of career opportunities occurs by enhancement of one's computer skills.
Revised
Career opportunities increase by enhancing one's computer skills.

Original
A stipulation by the admissions committee is that the forms be handed in by applicants no later than the first of December.
Revised
The admissions committee stipulates that applicants hand in the forms no later than the first of December.

An Editing Checklist for Conciseness and Clarity

★ Create strong verbs

Some verbs are weak in that they do not express a specific action. In contrast to using such weak verbs, a writer should use strong verbs such as **is**, **are**, **was**, **were**, **has**, **give**, **make**, **come** and **take** that imply a clear action. Consider the following examples:

如前單元所示，使用動詞使句子意念表現的更清晰，然而，有些動詞讓人感覺並不強勁，無法有力闡示一個動作。動詞如 **is, are, was, were, has, give, make, come,** 還有 **take** 等都屬此類。所以，作者應使用強有力的動詞來指明一個清楚的行爲。細想以下例句：

Original
The machine operator conducts transportation of the auto parts to the assembly line.
Revised
The machine operator transports the auto parts to the assembly line.

Original
The machine operator conducts transportation of the auto parts to the assembly line.

Revised
The machine operator transports the auto parts to the assembly line.

Original
The gross domestic product was not signfiicantly different between the two countries.
Revised
The two countries did not significantly differ in gross domestic product.

★ Avoid sentences beginning with *It* and *There*

Another form of wordiness and ambiguity is sentences beginning with ***There*** and ***It***. Unless ***It*** refers to a specific noun in the previous sentence, omit ***It is*** entirely. Consider the following examples:

使用 ***It*** 及 ***There*** 開頭的句子容易使文章語多累贅及曖昧不清。
除非 ***It*** 指的是先前句子所提特定的名詞，否則完全的避免 ***It is*** 的句型。

Original

There can be little doubt that ink jet printers have a higher per-page cost than laser printers.

Revised

Ink jet printers undoubtedly have a higher per-page cost than laser printers.

Original

It is important to develop a more effective approach to solve the complicated problem.

Revised

A more effective approach must be developed to solve the complicated problem.

Original

There is increasing evidence that supports the role of protein in prolonging life.

Revised

Increasing evidence supports the role of protein in prolonging life.

Original

It is necessary to examine exactly how nutrition affects growth.

Revised

Exactly how nutrition affects growth must be examined.

★ Delete redundant and needless phrases.

Many technical documents are cluttered with redundant or needless phrases that can be either deleted entirely or expressed more simply. The writer should try to avoid needless and redundant words and phrases that only make the sentence lengthy. Consider the following examples:

除去重複及不必要的措詞

這些擾人重複不必要的文詞其實可以完全去除，或是用更簡明的方式表達。作者若不注意這個細節則會使句子變得愈來愈長。細想以下例句：

Original

It is recommended by us that the trackball be selected on the occasion of purchasing a user interface device of this type.

Revised

We recommend selecting the trackball when purchasing a user interface device of this type.

Original
The trackball is deficient of the mobility that a mouse has despite the fact that the trackball requires less hand movement than the mouse.
Revised
The trackball lacks the mobility of a mouse although the former requires less hand movement than the latter.

Original
The web browser in all cases gives consideration to the user's needs in a situation in which he or she is away from the office.
Revised
The web browser always considers the user's needs when he or she is away from the office.

B. Clarity

★ Ensure subject and verb agreement

Subject and verb disagreement not only creates confusion over how many people, places or objects are involved, but also gives the sentence a faulty logic. A major reason for subject-verb disagreement is failing to recognize the subject and the verb. Consider the following examples:

如果主詞的單複數與動詞不能配合，不僅讀者感到困惑，同時句子的邏輯也會發生問題。

Original
Either the collected data set or two additional outputs was used to construct a neural network model.
Revised
Either the collected data set or two additional outputs were used to construct a neural network model.

Original
The research assistant and the doctoral candidate are the same person.
Revised
The research assistant and the doctoral candidate is the same person.

Original

Physics make most first year doctoral students nervous.

Revised

Physics makes most first year doctoral students nervous.

Original

The acoustics in the auditorium is excellent.

Revised

The acoustics in the auditorium are excellent.

★ Ensure that pronoun references are clear in meaning

Readers become confused when the sentences they are reading contain pronouns that do not have a clear antecedent. An antecedent is what a pronoun is referring to. Many problems can arise when a pronoun does not refer to a clear antecedent. Consider the following examples:

如果代名詞所指的人物或事物不能交待清楚，也是徒增讀者困惑。

Original

When a decision reaches the final stage, it must be implemented promptly.

Revised

When reaching the final stage, a decision must be implemented promptly.

Or

A decision must be implemented promptly when reaching the final stage.

Original

No adjustment factors exist if (C1) is violated, which implies that the transformation approach can be implemented.

Revised

The fact that no adjustment factors exist if (C1) is violated implies that the transformation approach can be implemented.

Or

No adjustment factors exist if (C1) is violated, implying that the transformation approach can be implemented.

Or

No adjustment factors exist if (C1) is violated; this violation implies that the transformation can be implemented.

Original

Driving a car and talking on a cellular phone at the same time is dangerous; this could cause an accident.

Revised

Driving a car and talking on a cellular phone at the same time is dangerous; this habit could cause an accident.

★ Create sentences parallel in structure and meaning

Parallelism in writing means that all parts of a sentence must have a similar construction. Consider the following examples:

科技英文寫作中，句子的建構必須有一致性。

Original

The numerical example concentrates mainly on illustration of the cases derived in the previous section and demonstrating the effectiveness of the proposed model.

Revised

The numerical example illustrates the cases derived in the previous section and demonstrates the effectiveness of the proposed model.

Original

The committee made a decision to set a new agenda and that the meeting should be adjourned.

Revised

The committee decided to set a new agenda and adjourn the meeting.

Original

The robust design focuses not only on collecting data accumulated from the designed experiment, but also that the results obtained by using Taguchi's two-step procedure are compared.

Revised

The robust design focuses not only on collecting data accumulated from the designed experiment, but also on comparing the results obtained by using Taguchi's two-step procedure.

Original

The proposed project is promising, creative, and has innovative ideas.

Revised

The proposed project is promising, creative, and innovative.

★ Eliminate modifier problems

As a word, phrase, or clause, a modifier describes another word, phrase, or clause. The reader becomes confused when the modifying clause or phrase is not next to the word it modifies. This often creates a gap between the author's intended meaning and what is actually written. Consider the following examples:

修飾語必須放在所要修飾的字之旁。

Original
To keep in shape, exercise is a must for an athlete.
Revised
An athlete must exercise to keep in shape.

Original
When an engineer, customer satisfaction should be attempted.
Revised
An engineer should attempt to satisfy the customer.

Original
After simulating a real environment, a consensus was reached.
Revised
After the researchers simulated a real environment, a consensus was reached.

Original
Being radioactive, the technician handled the materials with extreme care.
Revised
The technician handled the radioactive materials with extreme care.

★ Double check for faulty comparisons and omissions

Sentences that contain comparisons that are illogical and incomplete create further ambiguity in technical writing. Editors must also recognize words that have been carelessly omitted. Consider the following examples:

不合邏輯及不完整的比較詞造成更多的含糊不清，同時注意不小心漏掉的字。

Original

Our algorithm is more accurate with respect to computational time.

Revised

Our algorithm is more accurate than conventional ones with respect to computational time.

Original

The chemistry department cooperates with local industry more than their department.

Revised

The chemistry department cooperates with local industry more than their department does.

Original

The novel material is as strong, if not stronger than, available ones.

Revised

The novel material is as strong as, if not stronger than, available ones.

Original

The research department's productivity is higher than the administrative division.

Revised

The research department's productivity is higher than that of the administrative division.

★ Avoid unnecessary shifts in a sentence

Another obstacle to clarity in technical writing is unnecessary shifts in subject, tense, voice and mood.

作者應避免句中不必要的主詞，時態及語態之轉換。

Original

Communicators must share a common language or protocol so that we can easily understand each other.

Revised

Communicators must share a common language or protocol so that they can easily understand each other.

Original

A computer mouse needs some available workspace and even the beginning user can operate them with very little difficulty.

Revised

A computer mouse needs some available workspace and even the beginning user can operate one with very little difficulty.

Original

Execute the program commands and the iteration steps must be repeated.

Revised

Execute the program commands and repeat the iteration steps.

Original

The supervisor asked her employees if the assignment was ready and could it be handed in tomorrow.

Revised

The supervisor asked her employees if the assignment was ready and could be handed in tomorrow.

Useful phrases in an effective study plan

If admitted to your program, I intend to concentrate on…

In addition to a distinguished program in________, your renowned research in __________ is widely recognized. This explains why I chose ______ University for Doctoral studies.

My strong academic performance and solid background in _________ and strong academic performance has prepared me to meet the rigorous challenges of your program.

I would like to build upon my solid academic training and relevant work experiences by pursuing a Ph. d. in…

During my upcoming graduate studies, I look forward to absorbing enormous amounts of new information that is not related directly to my course requirements.

I am interested in answering these questions in Graduate school.

I have decided to pursue a graduate degree in…

My graduate school research will hopefully center on…

I plan to identify…

I intend to actively participate in…

Thus, I wish to further my knowledge through Graduate studies on _________research, which is a timely topic for the ___________sector in Taiwan.

From an early age, I have had much enthusiasm in…

These exciting times in the _______field fuel my aspiration to attain a Ph.D. in _______ as a logical basis with which to undertake a career in related research.

This explains why I have decided to devote myself to effectively addressing…

The strong research fundamentals acquired during my undergraduate years at ______ Chi University have prepared me for advanced study in __________.

I believe that my creativity and unique perspectives will contribute positively to any research team, regardless of whether we are engaging in case studies or undertaking research projects.

The _____________program at your prestigious school offers a starting point in my search to effectively address this obstacle.

With my desire to pursue advanced study in this area, several professors in my department recommended your school owing to its excellent faculty and research environment.

I hope to refine my writing and presentation skills through the design of a similar work during graduate study.

I not only learned the mechanics of writing a research paper, but also became aware of my lack of adequate knowledge in properly designing a study, evaluating data, and communicating my results orally. I believe that these skills are essential for researchers in this field.

Actively participating in each stage of the project, from original concept formation and experimental process design to experimental implementation, not only improved my research skills but also broadened my knowledge base.

Notably, when difficulties were encountered during my experiments, I was motivated to strive for successful results.

After passing a highly competitive nationwide entrance examination, I was admitted to the __________Department at ________University in 1999 where I majored in ________.

This solid undergraduate training has prepared me for the rigorous demands of advanced study in this field.

Several academic awards attest to the strong analytical skills and research fundamentals that I developed in order to conduct related research.

My transcripts indicate that, as I became more comfortable and at ease with my new life as a college student, my grades gradually improved each semester.

Department courses were particularly effective in fostering my ability to solve problems logically.

Although limited resources and facilities prevented me from an in depth investigation, theoretical knowledge and practical laboratory experiences furthered my interest in this field.

A sound academic background in ________ at ___________University, has provided me with the fundamental skills required for advanced research.

Useful phrases in an effective study plan

Coursework heavily emphasized practical applications, often providing me with many opportunities to come into contact with numerous enterprises.

In addition to theoretical study, I have emerged myself in hands-on experiences that fostered my creativity and enabled me to apply my academic knowledge to the industrial sector.

The project instilled in me the importance of collaborative teamwork and the ability to coordinate individuals in a group effort.

My studies provided me with solid background knowledge as well as the desire to become an academic researcher in this exciting field.

These achievements reaffirm my determination to pursue further studies so that I will have studies, which will provide me with the necessary professional skills for my future career.

This experience reinforced my dedication to laboratory work and stressed the significance of developing pertinent research questions and experimental designs, which facilitate data analysis.

In addition to my academic background, I have excelled in information technology-related skills, such as

In addition to nurturing my problem-solving skills and advanced knowledge in this field, the above experiences have sharpened my ability to define specific situations, think logically, collect related information, and analyze problems independently.

I thoroughly enjoy this research discipline, particularly the complete process of forming a construct, rendering a hypothesis, clarifying minute aspects and receiving critical comments from other researchers.

These experiences have exposed me to the dynamic nature of related investigations and the exciting challenges of a research career.

I am prepared to immerse myself in Academia and believe that I have the intellect and determination to satisfy its challenges.

This research strengthened my commitment to____________, which I intended to pursue during my Doctoral studies at your university.

Participating in numerous activities has helped me nurture leadership and collaborative skills, which are essential to my future aims.
Collaborative experiences from extracurricular activities during my undergraduate degree have enabled

me to effectively communicate with research associates that have diverse academic backgrounds.

In addition to the knowledge gained through coursework, I also collaborated with others in numerous extracurricular activities.

In addition to studying diligently and maintaining a solid academic record, I have balanced my professional life with a diverse range of extracurricular activities.

This unique leadership opportunity has been one of the most rewarding experiences of my undergraduate years.

This diverse experience strengthened and broadened my solid knowledge base, and further enhanced my sensitivity towards various related issues.

While increasing my interest in communications, this experience also reaffirmed my ability to achieve my career goals by applying my knowledge skills systematically.

The numerous extracurricular activities that I participated in during university gave me the necessary balance of developing academic and social skills simultaneously.

I view disappointments and trials as an opportunity to learn and, thus, strengthen my personal stamina.

My previous academic performance and related experiences reflect my strong determination to pursue an advance degree in________________.

Graduate school will provide me with many opportunities to collaborate and interact with classmates and professors, as well as occasionally meeting with entrepreneurs. These are situations in which I am highly competent.

My colleagues and superiors can attest to my responsible and trustworthy character.

I am confident that I can contribute positively to collaborative efforts in graduate school.

Despite the occasional frustrations of daily life, I have maintained an optimistic attitude as reflected by my person ambition to pursue a research career in Academia.

I have decided to devote my career to researching…

After completing a Masters degree in_____ from your university, I will return to Taiwan prepared to make a significant contribution.

Combining work experiences with a Master's degree, I hope to eventually attain a managerial position.

Despite my solid academic training, I still feel somewhat unprepared for the workplace, particularly a managerial position.

By acquiring advanced knowledge and specialized skills that your program offers, I will be well equipped and more confident to manage such a position.

I am convinced that the professional training from your university will provide me with numerous opportunities to put my knowledge and skills to deserving use.

I believe that completing the graduate program at your university is the only way to fully realize my career aspirations.

Earning a Graduate degree from your prestigious institution would fully prepare me for a career in the ________ sector.

I believe that Graduate education in your country would fully equip me with the latest skills required to thrive in this highly competitive field.

Fully aware of the graduate curricula and academic expectations at your university, I feel that this institution is the best place to fully realize my goals.

Your university's excellent academic environment will allow me to achieve the goals I have created for myself.

I am particularly drawn to your programs that focus on equipping its graduates with the technical competence and flexibility necessary to respond effectively to challenges within that profession.

I believe that I have the talent, insight, intelligence, creativity, and potential to contribute to the rich pool of talented individuals at your university.

What attracted me most to your university was the highly qualified and experienced faculty with frequent publications in prestigious journals, seemingly unlimited academic resources, as well as its distinctive and unique tradition.

Graduate study is the logical next step to fully realizing my career potential.

Graduate study in your country would equip me with the skills necessary to thrive in the workplace.

To achieve my career aspirations, I intend to enhance my education through the graduate program at your university.

The solid graduate curricula program at your university will build upon and refine the fundamental skills that I gained during undergraduate study.

I decided to go abroad for graduate school not only to further develop my knowledge, skills, but also to gain invaluable experiences that will benefit my future work and enrich my life.

About the Author and Acknowledgments

Born on his father's birthday, (September 20, 1965), Ted Knoy received a Bachelor of Arts in History at Franklin College of Indiana (Franklin, Indiana) and a Masters of Public Administration at American International College (Springfield, Massachusetts). He is currently a Ph.d student in Education at the University of East Anglia (Norwich, England). Having conducted research and independent study in South African, India, Nicaragua, and Switzerland, he has lived in Taiwan since 1989 where he is a permanent resident.

An associate researcher at Union Chemical Laboratories (Industrial Technology Research Institute), Ted is also a technical writing instructor at the Department of Computer Science, National Tsing Hua University as well as the Institute for Information Management and the Department of Communications Engineering, National Chiao Tung University. He is also the English editor of several technical and medical journals in Taiwan.

Ted is author of the Chinese Technical Writers Series, which includes An English Style Approach for Chinese Technical Writers, English Oral Presentations for Chinese Technical Writers, A Correspondence Manual for Chinese Technical Writers, An Editing Workbook for Chinese Technical Writers, and Advanced Copyediting Practice for Chinese Technical Writers.

Ted created and coordinates the Chinese OWL (On-line Writing Lab) at http://mx.nthu.edu.tw/~tedknoy

Acknowledgments

Thanks to Yang Jin Yao for the illustrations in this book. Thanks also to my technical writing students in the Department of Computer Science at National Tsing Hua University, as well as in the Institute of Information Management, Department of Communication Engineering, and Department of Information Science at National Chiao Tung University. Professor Tong Lee-Eeng of the Department of Industrial Management at National Chiao Tung University is appreciated for the use of her materials. Tamara Reynish and Seamus Harris are also appreciated for reviewing this workbook.

科技英文寫作系列之一

精通科技論文(報告)寫作之捷徑

An English Style Approach For Chinese Technical Writers （修訂版）

作者：柯泰德（Ted Knoy）

內容簡介

使用直接而流利的英文會話
讓您所寫的英文科技論文很容易被了解
提供不同形式的句型供您參考利用
比較中英句子結構之異同
利用介系詞片語將二個句子連接在一起

萬其超／ 李國鼎科技發展基金會秘書長

本書是多年實務經驗和專注力之結晶，因此是一本坊間少見而極具實用價值的書。

陳文華／ 國立清華大學工學院院長

中國人使用英文寫作時，語法上常會犯錯，本書提供了很好的實例示範，對於科技論文寫作有相當參考價值。

徐　章／ 工業技術研究院量測中心主任

這是一個讓初學英文寫作的人，能夠先由不犯寫作的錯誤開始再根據書中的步驟逐步學習提升寫作能力的好工具， 此書的內容及解說方式使讀者也可以無師自通，藉由自修的方式學習進步，但是更重要的是它雖然是一本好書，當您學會了書中的許多技巧，如果您還想要更進步，那麼基本原則還是要常常練習，才能發揮書中的精髓。

Kathleen Ford, English Editor, Proceedings(Life Science Divison), National Science Council

The Chinese Technical Writers Series is valuable for anyone involved with creating scientific documentation.

※若有任何英文文件修改問題，請直接與柯泰德先生聯絡：(03) 5724895

特　價　新台幣300元
劃　撥　19419482 清蔚科技股份有限公司
線上訂購　四方書網　www.4Book.com.tw
發行所　華香園出版社

科技英文寫作系列之二

作好英文會議簡報

English presentations for Chinese Technical Writers

作者：柯泰德（Ted Knoy）

內容簡介

本書共分十二個單元，涵括產品開發、組織、部門、科技、及產業的介紹、科技背景、公司訪問、研究能力及論文之發表等，每一單元提供不同型態的科技口頭簡報範例，以進行英文口頭簡報的寫作及表達練習，是一本非常實用的著作。

李鍾熙／ 工業技術研究院化學工業研究所所長

一個成功的科技簡報，就是使演講流暢，用簡單直接的方法、清楚表達內容。本書提供一個創新的方法(途徑)，給組織每一成員做爲借鏡，得以自行準備口頭簡報。利用本書這套有系統的方法加以練習，將必然使您信心備增，簡報更加順利成功。

薛敬和／ IUPAC 台北國際高分子研討會執行長
國立清華大學教授

本書以個案方式介紹各英文會議簡報之執行方式，深入簡出，爲邁入實用狀況的最佳參考書籍。

沙晉康／ 清華大學化學研究所所長
第十五屆國際雜環化學會議主席

本書介紹英文簡報的格式，値得國人參考。今天在學術或工商界與外國接觸來往均日益增多，我們應加強表達的技巧，尤其是英文的簡報應具有很高的專業手準。本書做爲一個很好的範例。

張俊彥／ 國立交通大學電機資訊學院教授兼院長

針對中國學生協助他們寫好英文的國際論文和參加國際會議如何以英語演講、內容切中要害特別推薦。

※若有任何英文文件修改問題，請直接與柯泰德先生聯絡：(03) 5724895

科技英文寫作系列之三

英文信函參考手冊

A Correspondence Manual for Chinese Technical Writers

作者：柯泰德（Ted Knoy）

內容簡介

本書期望成爲從事專業管理與科技之中國人，在國際場合上溝通交流時之參考指導書籍。本書所提供的書信範例（附磁碟片），可爲您撰述信件時的參考範本。更實際的是，本書如同一「寫作計畫小組」，能因應特定場合（狀況）撰寫出所需要的信函。

李國鼎／ 總統府資政

我國科技人員在國際場合溝通表達之機會急遽增加，希望大家都來重視英文說寫之能力。

羅明哲／ 國立中興大學教務長

一份表達精準且適切的英文信函，在國際間的往來交流上，重要性不亞於研究成果的報告發表。本書介紹各類英文技術信函的特徵及寫作指引，所附範例中肯實用，爲優良的學習及參考書籍。

廖俊臣／ 國立清華大學理學院院長

本書提供許多有關工業技術合作、技術轉移、工業資訊、人員訓練及互訪等接洽信函的例句和範例，頗爲實用，極具參考價值。

于樹偉／ 工業安全衛生技術發展中心主任

國際間往來日益頻繁，以英文有效地溝通交流，是現今從事科技研究人員所需具備的重要技能。本書在寫作風格、文法結構與取材等方面，提供極佳的寫作參考與指引，所列舉的範例，皆經過作者細心的修訂與潤飾，必能切合讀者的實際需要。

※若有任何英文文件修改問題，請直接與柯泰德先生聯絡：(03) 5724895

特　價　新台幣250元

劃　撥　19419482 清蔚科技股份有限公司

線上訂購　四方書網 www.4Book.com.tw

發行所　工業技術研究院

科技英文寫作系列之四

科技英文編修訓練手冊

An Editing Workbook For Chinese Technical Writers

作者：柯泰德（Ted Knoy）

內容簡介

要把科技英文寫的精確並不是件容易的事情。通常在投寄文稿發表前，作者都要前前後後修改草稿，在這樣繁複過程中甚至最後可能請專業的文件編修人士代勞雕琢使全文更爲清楚明確。

本書由科技論文的寫作型式、方法型式、內容結構及內容品質著手，並以習題方式使學生透過反覆練習熟能生巧，能確實提昇科技英文之寫作及編修能力。

劉炯朗／ 國立清華大學校長

「科技英文寫作」式一項非常重要的技巧。本書針對台灣科技研究人員在英文寫作發表這方面的訓練，書中以實用性練習對症下藥，期望科技英文寫作者熟能生巧，實在是一個很有用的教材。

彭旭明／ 國立台灣大學副校長

本書爲科技英文寫作系列之四；以練習題爲主，由反覆練習中提昇寫作及編輯能力。適合理、工、醫、農的學生及研究人員使用，特爲推薦。

許千樹／ 國立交通大學研究發展處研發長

處於今日高科技時代，國人用到科技英文寫作之機會甚多，如何能以精練的手法寫出一篇好的科技論文，極爲重要。本書針對國人寫作之缺點提供了各種清楚的編修範例，實用性高，極具參考價值。

陳文村／ 國立清華大學電機資訊學院院長

處在我國日益國際化、資訊化的社會裡，英文書寫是必備的能力，本書提供很多極具參考價值的範例。柯泰德先生在清大任教科技英文寫作多年，深受學生喜愛，本人樂於推薦此書。

國家圖書館出版品預行編目資料

有效撰寫英文讀書計畫 / Writing Effective Study Plans

柯泰德(Ted Knoy)作 —初版—

新竹市：清蔚科技，2001【民90】

面；21x29.7公分(應用英文寫作系列；1)

ISBN 957-97544-6-2 (平裝)

1.英國語言 - 寫作法 2.論文寫作法

805.17 90006677

應用英文系列 1

有效撰寫英文讀書計畫

作　　者／柯泰德(Ted Knoy)

發 行 人／徐明哲

法律顧問／志揚國際法律事務所

發 行 所／清蔚科技股份有限公司

網　　址／http://www.4Book.com.tw

電子郵件／4Book@CWEB.com.tw

地　　址／300 新竹市光復路二段 101 號　國立清華大學創新育成中心 301 室

電　　話／03-574-1023
《如果您對本書品質與服務有任何不滿意的地方，請打這支電話》

傳　　真／03-574-1021

印 刷 所／沈氏藝術印刷股份有限公司

美術設計／陳偉婷

版　　次／2001 年 6 月 初版

國際書碼／ISBN 957-97544-6-2

建議售價／450 元

劃撥帳號／帳戶　清蔚科技股份有限公司

帳號　19419482